# 情在贵州山水间

◆ 叶辛

贵州出版集团
贵州人民出版社

图书在版编目（CIP）数据

情在贵州山水间 / 叶辛著 . -- 贵阳：贵州人民出版社，2025.4. -- ISBN 978-7-221-18507-5

Ⅰ．I267

中国国家版本馆 CIP 数据核字第 20244R2P93 号

## 情在贵州山水间
Love in the Mountains and Rivers of Guizhou

叶辛　著

---

| | |
|---|---|
| 顾　　问 | 李汉宇　顾　久 |
| 选题策划 | 孔祥柱　刘学文　张云端 |
| 策划编辑 | 张云端 |
| 责任编辑 | 程林骁　刘向辉 |
| 英文翻译 | 张庆旸 |
| 作品推广 | 贵商总会　天下贵州人活动组委会　叶辛好花红书院<br>叶辛荔波文学院　贵州光阴故事文化发展有限公司 |
| 装帧设计 | 狮扬文化 |
| 文创设计 | 元典文化 |
| 出版发行 | 贵州出版集团　贵州人民出版社 |
| 地　　址 | 贵阳市观山湖区中天会展城会展东路 SOHO 公寓 A 座 |
| 印　　刷 | 天津睿和印艺科技有限公司 |
| 版　　次 | 2025 年 4 月第 1 版 |
| 印　　次 | 2025 年 4 月第 1 次印刷 |
| 开　　本 | 787 毫米 x1092 毫米　1/32 |
| 印　　张 | 10 |
| 字　　数 | 420 千字 |
| 书　　号 | ISBN 978-7-221-18507-5 |
| 定　　价 | 68.00 元 |

---

如发现图书印装质量问题，请与印刷厂联系调换；版权所有，翻版必究；未经许可，不得转载。

# 编者的话

2024年全国两会期间，贵州省委主要领导以"黄小西吃晚饭"这一亲切而富有诗意的方式，向世人推荐了贵州的绝美景色，不仅展现了贵州人的热情好客，更激发了无数人对这片神秘土地的好奇与向往。"黄小西吃晚饭"已然成为了贵州旅游的新名片，它不仅仅是一句风趣的口头禅，更是贵州人民对这片土地深沉热爱的升华，以及对打造世界级旅游目的地坚定信念的传递。

贵州这片神奇而多彩土地，山川壮丽，风光旖旎，自古以来便是文人墨客笔下的灵感源泉。叶辛作为中国当代著名作家，以其独特的视角和深邃的情感，长期关注并书写着"第二故乡"贵州的山山水水、风土人情。他的文字，如同山间清泉，潺潺流淌，不仅让人领略到黄果树瀑布的磅礴气势、小七孔景区的灵秀多姿、西江苗寨的古老神秘、赤水丹霞的瑰丽多彩、万峰林的壮阔雄浑以及梵净山的清幽圣洁，更引领读者走进贵州人民丰富多彩的生活世界，感受那份淳朴与热情。为了深入展现贵州的自然之美、人文之韵,我们在叶辛众多的描写贵州山水、人文、风情散文中,以"黄小西吃晚饭"为切入口,精心策划编选了叶辛这本散文集——《情在贵州山水间》。

在这本散文集中,叶辛以细腻的笔触描绘了贵州的自然景观,同时也深入挖掘了贵州的文化底蕴和民族风情。无论是黄果树瀑布前的驻足凝望,还是小七孔桥上的漫步遐思;无论是西江苗寨的苗家盛宴,还是赤水河畔的渔舟唱晚;无论是万峰林下的田园牧歌,还是梵净山顶的禅意人生,都被叶辛赋予了新的生命和意义。

我们相信,这本散文集将成为广大读者了解贵州、走进贵州、爱上贵州的重要窗口。它不仅能够让读者在文字间领略到贵州的自然风光和人文魅力,更能够激发人们对美好生活的向往和追求。让我们跟随叶辛的脚步,去感受"黄小西吃晚饭"背后的贵州魅力,去探寻那些隐藏在山水之间的美丽故事。

# 情深意切

◆ 叶辛

2019年,共和国成立70周年,贵州人民出版社出版了我的长篇小说《五姐妹》,作为献礼新中国成立70周年的作品。

也是在同一年,吉林人民出版社,出版了我的一本散文集《我和祖国70年》,吉林省也把这本书列为新中国成立70年的作品。

仿佛都是昨天的事。转眼之际,又是5年过去了。今年,新中国成立75周年了,贵州人民出版社出版了我这本《情在贵州山水间》的散文集,我的心中,同样把这本书,作为一个作家对新中国75周年的献礼。

和今年同样要由北京与上海出版社出版的长篇小说五卷本及散文集而言,《情在贵州山水间》写的是贵州的山水散文、人文散文、民族散文、风情散文。这些都和已经与我结缘了55年的贵州省有关。

随着贵州省在这些年中旅游文化事业的发展,贵州的山

水和风情已经逐渐为世人所知并获得赞许。

无论在省外的哪些地方,话题只要涉及贵州,都会有人道,"贵州这些年来真的干得不错""贵州的风景美得令人惊讶""我去过一次,以后还想去"等等。

不过,我得讲一句实话,旅游毕竟是旅游,哪怕在一地待上个一天、两天,乃至几天,游客们对于秀美风光,各地的人文地理,乃至历史典故及趣闻,所得到的印象终究还是浮光掠影的。比如世人都知道的黄果树瀑布,是如何逐渐被人认识的?挨着广西的荔波小七孔景区,其特点是啥?近十几年的黔东南西江苗寨,怎么保存得如此完好,吸引来那么多的客人?

还有几乎可与黄果树瀑布媲美的赤水大瀑布，为何却鲜为人知？黔西南兴义的万峰林，瑰丽的风光让人迷醉，又该如何欣赏？被评上世界自然遗产以后天天人满为患的梵净山，一年四季有什么不同……

近五年里我重游这些景点和景区，又有了一些对比和思考，结合半个多世纪以来我对贵州山地上人和物的认识和理解，我写下了一篇篇散文。恰逢新中国成立75周年，把这些赞颂黔山秀水的文字配上照片编成一本散文集，也相信会对人们进一步认识贵州，理解贵州，热爱贵州起一点作用。

文短意长，是为序。

2024年5月于孔学堂

梵净山蘑菇石

# True and Sincere

◆ Ye Xin

In 2019, the 70th anniversary of the founding of the People's Republic of China, Guizhou People's Publishing House published my novel *Five Sisters* as a tribute to the 70th anniversary of the founding of the People's Republic of China.

In the same year, Jilin People's Publishing House published a collection of my essays *70 Years of My Life with the Motherland*. Jilin Province also listed this book as a work to celebrate the 70th anniversary of the founding of the People's Republic of China.

It seems like yesterday. Another five years have passed. This year is the 75th anniversary of the founding of the People's Republic of China. Guizhou People's Publishing House has published my collection of essays entitled *Love in the Mountains and Rivers of Guizhou*. As a writer, I also regard this book as a gift for the 75th anniversary of the founding of the People's Republic of China.

For the five-volume novel and prose collection, which will also be published in Beijing and Shanghai this year, *Love in the Mountains and Rivers of Guizhou* is written in Guizhou, including landscape proses, humanistic proses, ethnic proses, and customs proses. All of these proses are related to Guizhou

Province, which has been my bond for 55 years.

With the development of cultural tourism in Guizhou in recent years, Guizhou's landscape and customs have gradually become widely known and praised by the world.

No matter in any province in China, if you talk about Guizhou, someone will say, "Guizhou has really done well these years!" "The scenery in Guizhou is surprisingly beautiful!" "I went once, and I want to go again!"...

However, I have to tell the truth, tourism is just tourism, even if you stay in a place for a day, two days, or even a few days, the tourists will get a shallow impression of the scenery, people, geography, historical allusions and anecdotes. For example, the well-known Huangguoshu Waterfall, how is it gradually recognized by people? Xiaoqikong scenic spot in Libo, what are its characteristics? How can the Xijiang Miao Village in southeast Guizhou in recent ten years be preserved so well? Attracting so many guests?

Also, about Chishui Waterfall, why is not well-known? Xingyi Wanfenglin the magnificent scenery makes people enchanted, and how to appreciate it? After being assessed as a World Natural Heritage site, Fanjing Mountain is crowded every day, what is the difference in the four seasons...

In the past five years, I have visited these scenic spots again, made some comparisons and reflections, and combined with my knowledge and understanding of people and things in Guizhou over the past half century, I have written a series of essays. Coincining with the 75th anniversary of the founding of New China, compiling these words and photos to celebrate the landscape into a collection of essays will also play a role in people's further knowledge, understanding and love of Guizhou.

Brief but meaningful — this serves as the preface.

黄果树瀑布附近的布依族石头寨

# 译者话

◆ 张庆旸

在中国乃至亚洲地区，大多数读者提到叶辛老师更多的是讨论他所获得的荣誉以及各种头衔；尽管这些名誉让叶老师被众人所熟知；但是叶老师的第一重身份是作家，因此，此译者将会着重探讨叶老师的写作内容，写作背景，以及译者作为千禧年一代是如何鉴赏叶老师作品的。

2024年初，中国香港著名导演王家卫的首部电视剧《繁花》在中国受到了极大的关注，而讨论点之一是《繁花》为近年来的第二部用上海话演绎的电视剧，著名演员马伊琍在接受采访时说："在她印象中，上一部用上海话演绎的电视剧还是由叶老师同名小说改编的《孽债》。"一段时间内《孽债》又一次成为了文艺以及电影行业专家津津乐道的话题。近些年来，随着越来越多的外地人来上海定居，会说上海话的人越来越少，上海话不再像二十多年前那样听闻于各个弄堂间，《孽债》和《繁花》这两部电视剧使得越来越多的年轻人学习了解并且开始作为一种媒介传播上海话以及上海文化。叶老师的《孽债》无疑是在这个上海话逐渐被年轻一代人所遗忘的时代让上海文化重回大众视野，这是上海话以及沪文化的传播在近些年来的巨大进步。

叶老师作为一个上海人，一直以独特的视角在讲述中国20世纪80年代前城市知识青年前往欠发达地区或者山区传授知识以及参与劳作的故事。在中国的历史教材中我们只能对这一段时间发生的故事略知一二，甚至很难知晓在这其中的历史背景，而叶老师以第一人称视角带我们走入这一段历史，了解他的故事以及他在这一段岁月里的真切感悟。对于我们21世纪00年代出生的年轻人而言，通过叶老师讲述的故事才能更好的了解这一段往事并且作为一种对历史的补充学习。这是叶老师作为一个历史传播者作出的成就。

以文学作品爱好者的视角鉴赏叶老师的作品通常会有很深刻的感悟。区别于"华丽派作者"倾向于使用夸张的修辞手法以及欲扬先抑的写作手法并加以华丽辞藻修饰来打动读者，叶老师的作品则更像是一部纪录片。叶老师从自己的故事开始描绘历史故事，文字更加容易理解并且故事的叙事性更为强烈，尤其是本书中对贵州山河风景的描绘更是形象生动，仿佛身临其境。同时在这些故事中穿插着对于现实的反映以及对于社会的思考，这些元素增强了真实感以及故事的多元化。

本书做英文翻译的初心在于让叶老师的书带着往事以及贵州山水走向世界，让更多外来游客以及国际上的文学爱好者有机会了解到故事发生的背景、贵州山水与风情以及深厚的文化底蕴；同时也是一个让更多喜爱中华文化的国际友人在字里行间体会贵州的人文风俗的契机。"中国灵魂，国际视野"是当代社会一直所讨论的，让精彩的故事和承载着历史的山水在国际上大放光彩是图书出版的使命以及意义所在！

以此祝愿每一位拿到这本书的读者带着一颗好奇的心，倾听叶老师所讲述的故事。

# Translator's preface

◆ Zhang Qingyang

In China and even the Asian region, most of the discussion about Ye Xin is about the honors and titles he has received. While these reputations have made Mr. Ye widely known, Mr. Ye's first identity is as a writer. Therefore, this translator's introduction will focus on the content of Mr. Ye's writing, the backstory, and how the translator, as a millennial, appreciates Mr. Ye's work.

In early 2024, Famous Hong Kong, China director Wong Kar-wai's first TV series *Blossoms Shanghai* has received a lot of attention in China. One of the points of discussion is that *Blossoms Shanghai* is the second TV series with Shanghainese in recent years. Famous actress Ma Yili said in an interview: In her impression, the last TV series with Shanghainese was *Nie Zhai* adapted from Mr. Ye's novel of the same name. For a period of time, *Nie Zhai* once again became a topic of interest for experts in literature and film industry. In recent years, with more and more foreigners coming to settle in Shanghai, there are fewer and fewer people who speak Shanghainese. Shanghainese is no longer heard in every alley as it was twenty years ago. The two TV series

*Nie Zhai* and *Blossoms Shanghai* make more and more young people learn about Shanghainese and start to spread Shanghainese culture as a medium. Mr. Ye's *Nie Zhai* undoubtedly brings Shanghai culture back to the public's attention in this era when Shanghainese is gradually forgotten by the younger generation, which is an achievement made by Mr. Ye as a disseminator of Shanghainese and Shanghai culture.

As a Shanghai native, Mr. Ye has been telling the story of Chinese urban educated youth who went to underdeveloped areas or mountainous areas to teach knowledge and participate in labor from a unique perspective before 1980s. In Chinese history textbooks, we can only know a little about the story that happened during this period, and it is even difficult to know the historical background in this period. However, Mr. Ye takes us into this period of history from the first-person perspective to understand his story and his real perception during this period. The translator, as a young man born in the 2000s, has a better understanding of this past event through the story told by Mr. Ye and serves as a supplementary study of history. This is Mr Ye's achievement as a historical communicator.

As a lover of literary works, I usually have a deep understanding of Mr. Ye's works from the perspective of appreciation. Whereas "pompous writers" tend to use exaggerated rhetorical devices and writing techniques to impress readers and embellish essays with flowery words, Mr. Ye's work is more like a documentary. Mr. Ye draws the historical story from his own story, making the text easier to understand and the story more narrative. In particular, the description of Guizhou mountains and rivers in the book is vivid and lifelike. These stories are interspersed with Mr. Ye's reflections on reality and society, which enhance the sense of reality and diversity of the stories.

The original intention of the English translation of this book is to let Mr. Ye's book bring the past events and Guizhou landscape to the world, so that more foreign tourists and international literature lovers have the opportunity to understand the background of the story, Guizhou landscape and scenery, and profound cultural heritage; At the same time, it is also an opportunity for more international friends who love Chinese culture to experience the humanistic customs of Guizhou between the lines. "Chinese soul, international vision" has been discussed in the contemporary society, so that the wonderful story and the landscape carrying history in the international glory is the mission and significance of book publishing !

With this as a preface, I hope that readers will listen to the story told by Mr. Ye with a curious heart!

# 目录

- 1     黄果树的歌
- 11    黄果树的彩虹
- 15    双挂大瀑布
- 19    黄果树协奏曲
- 29    神曲小七孔
- 33    小七孔的喧
- 43    弦歌四季的西江
- 49    西江华彩路
- 63    烟雨西江
- 71    镇远夜梦幻曲
- 75    赤水瀑布欢乐颂
- 81    春天的赤水河谷
- 89    万峰林乐章
- 97    云天独奏梵净山

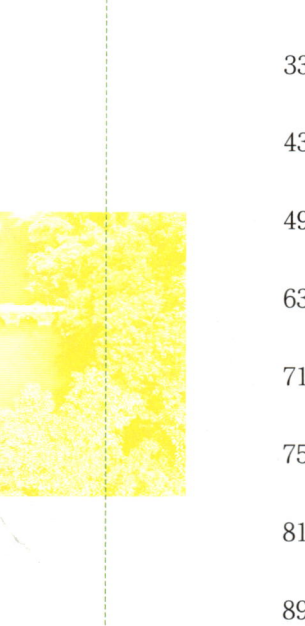

109　人间最短的河

113　该爱吗？

119　万彩的水

129　醉歌六月六

135　加油和安龙

141　我写贵州山水

145　金彩妥乐村

# 黄果树的歌

25年前,刚从贵州调回上海工作,写过一篇《黄果树瀑布群落》的小文,告诉上海读者的是,黄果树不仅仅是那一挂人们常在照片上看到的大瀑布。有名有姓的瀑布,对外开辟成景点的,就有九挂。而一般游客,去一趟贵州不容易,从省城贵阳挤出一整天时间,清早出门,游完黄果树大瀑布主要景点往回赶,也得天黑下来才能回到旅馆,是顾不上看其他群落的。故而,和黄果树有关的其他话题,我就没有展开写。

25年过去了,到贵州去旅游的客人越来越多,尤其是夏日,爽爽的贵阳以它独特的气候条件吸引着海内外的众多客人。贵州的老同事、熟人、文坛朋友们不止一次地告诉我,你要来,或是介绍朋友们来,一定要提前几周跟我们说,要不,好一点的旅馆都找不着。是啊,到了贵州的客人都要去黄果树走一走,看一看,回来之后就会盛赞黄果树的景观,啧啧称道龙宫的奇妙、漩塘的美丽、天星桥的令人流连。听着他们的评价和赞美,我自然高兴。高兴之余我又发现,他们看到的黄果树瀑布景区,还只是表面上的、浮泛的、一掠而过的。这自然无可厚非。但是,黄果树作为亚洲最大的瀑布,它的来历,它的历史,它多少世纪以来的变迁,它蕴含的文化品位,都是我们该知晓一二的。

我在《到多伦多会"情人"》一篇散文中写到美加边境的尼亚加拉大瀑布时提到一个细节,十九世纪的英国作家狄更斯游历过尼亚加拉瀑布,细读他留下的散文,会发现他当年看到的尼亚加拉瀑布,和我们今天看到的尼亚加拉大瀑布是不一样的,他曾经站立过的地方被冲刷成了河床,他不可能登上观光电梯,他也体验不到穿着塑料雨衣、坐着游艇冲击大瀑布的欢乐和惊险,他也没福气坐在旋转餐厅里边喝咖啡边远眺大瀑布的气势,他那个年代没有汽车,他是坐着马车去往尼亚加拉小镇,徒步绕着河岸观赏瀑布景观的……

说这一切,只是想说明,景点也是会随着时光而变迁的。我的这一篇时隔 25 年写下的小文,就是想告知读者一些鲜为人知的大瀑布的轶事。

### 黄果树瀑布没黄果

第一次去看黄果树大瀑布,是在上个世纪七十年代,农闲时节，和几个知青伙伴相约着，搭乘带篷的卡车去的。一路上匆匆忙忙，那个年头又没有今天人喝的纯净水、矿泉水，就有知青说，到了黄果树，买几只黄果来吃，解解渴。

贵州老乡所说的黄果，就是橙子和柑橘，我们想当然地以为，到了黄果树，黄果一定比别处的便宜，满街小摊上都能买到。

来到面对大瀑布的公路边，壮观的大瀑布是见着了，路边零星的小摊上，一只黄果也没见着。那个年头，没设景区，也不要门票，南来北往的车子，停下来就能观景。

渴得受不了的知青就哇哇大叫："奇了怪了，大名鼎鼎的黄果树，买不到一只黄果。"

老乡笑道："那是你憨，黄果树从来就没黄果。"

我问："这又是为何？"

老乡看我一脸认真，也答不出个所以然。

后来我多次去往黄果树，有几次还和作家们就在大瀑布附近住下来，几经探访，终于解开了这一谜团。黄果树这条河，古时称白水河。白水河两岸，不产柑橘和橙子，倒是有不少榕树。当地的各族老百姓，把大榕树称为黄葛树，故而在明朝之前，黄果树瀑布叫白水河瀑布、黄葛树瀑布。

由于黄葛树和黄果树音近，在贵州话里叫法几乎一样，久而久之，老百姓习惯成自然，黄果树瀑布的叫法就传开了。

清朝同治年间，约定俗成的叫法写了上去，大众战胜了小众，黄果树瀑布的叫法就固定下来，传播到全中国、全世界。正如同唐代诗人白居易，以通俗易懂的诗为人们所知，最终成为了中国文学家的典型代表。白诗千古流传，黄果树瀑布的名称，也因通俗而为历史所认同。

## 大瀑布的"痛"

黄果树瀑布的名声如此之大，但是它至今也未被评上世界自然遗产，不能不说这是大瀑布的"痛"。

进入新的世纪以来，贵州黔南的荔波、黔东南的云台山，都先后被评为世界自然遗产。而名声远远大于这两处的黄果树瀑布，却至今未申报，这又是何故呢？

1992年，黄果树兴致勃勃地要像其他全国著名的景点一样，准备"申遗"了，而且还把考察组请了来，结果事与愿违。联合国教科文组织的专家对黄果树考察之后，留下了一段评语："黄果树是亚洲最有影响的大瀑布，但同时人工痕迹太重，生态环境太差，建议暂缓申报'世界遗产'。"

人家说的是大实话。

黄果树得反省了。联合国派来的专家桑塞尔、卢卡斯在黄果树待了三天，在座谈会上，他们对黄果树"申遗"所做的大量工作和努力作了肯定，尤其强调了景点的科学价值、美学价值以及作为喀斯特演变重要例证的意义，对大瀑布、水帘洞、天然盆景园、天星洞、银链坠潭瀑布、水上石林等景点，更是看得十分高兴，不时露出笑容和伸出大拇指。

但是，车过半边街时，两位专家都叫停车子，下来不停地拍照。通过翻译，人们了解到他们说的是：景区过多地修建人为建筑是不对的。

这不对之处，包括黄果树发电站，包括在建的电站培训中心，包括溶涧的灯要安装隐蔽，不用彩灯……

半边街是最大的软肋。黄果树大瀑布飞溅弥漫的水珠、水沫和雾露，使得它的一侧山坡，终日笼罩在朦朦胧胧的湿重雾气之中，以至这半边山坡上的植物一年四季绿茵茵、鲜亮亮的，看去十分诱人，亦成了黄果树的一景。相反，面对着大瀑布的这半边山坡，既不会受到弥散而来的水雾水气的影响，更是眺望黄果树瀑布的最佳位置之一。老乡们就来这里摆摊设点，出售米粉、面条、包子、李子和各式的乡间小吃，特别是1982年，黄果树正式设立景区，修建了旅游观赏小道、公共厕所、宾馆设施，收取两角钱一张的门票。来自全国各地的游客越来越多，老乡们干脆就在这一最佳观瀑点修建起一个个饭馆、面铺、旅舍、茶馆、摄影点，逐渐形成了一条街。由于所有的建筑都修在这半边，人们自然而然把这条喧嚣、热闹、零乱、嘈杂、卫生条件也差的街，称作半边街。

桑塞尔、卢卡斯两位专家显然也对这条天天要路过的半边街印象深刻，拍下不少照片。到了北京之后，他们实话实说，提出了"暂缓申报"的建议。这给热切期待着申报遗产的黄果树人不啻是当头浇了一桶冷水。

冷静下来想想，人家也是在为黄果树大瀑布着想，因为按规定，每处景点只能申报一次，若被"世界自然遗产联盟"的21个常务理事国否定，便永远不能再申报了。贵州省建设厅和国家建设部，只得撤回了准备了好久的申报材料，争取治理好了环境再申报。

这一件事，不能不说是黄果树大瀑布的"痛"。这一痛，就痛了二十多年。

要写今日黄果树，得从我的一首小诗写起：

>  今日黄果树
> 
> 艳阳丽日黄果树，
> 
> 古时驿道成新路。
> 
> 七色彩虹迎瀑布，
> 
> 诱人绿坡拂雾露。

这是今年盛夏时节，我陪友人游览黄果树时即兴写下的。

那天阳光灿烂得带着几分喜气，黄果树的绿荫在蓝天白云的映衬下片片叶子都泛着亮光，我们顺着游览黄果树的最佳线路，从陡坡塘瀑布这里往下行。

这条线路，当年是五尺宽的古驿道。徐霞客那年春天，就是沿着这条古驿道，循声看见了陡坡塘瀑布景观的。他的原话是"瀑声震天，十里相闻"。这样的古驿道不常见了，景区把它们保护了起来，另外为游人们修了木质的栈道。

没有人想得到，这里曾是小摊林立的"半边街"。

沿着栈道漫步而行，白水河坦荡宽阔的流水逐渐收窄，水势悄然地形成一股丰盈膨胀的急流，湍急起来，迅捷起来，往前奔腾而泻。

凝神观赏，游客不难发现，黄果树大瀑布的壮观气势，就是从这里逐渐蓄积起来的。

几十年里，我游览过几十次黄果树了，阴雨天到过黄果树，大冬天到过黄果树，白天来过黄果树，夜间看过黄果树，春秋天游过黄果树，大雨天赏过黄果树如洪如涛的暴怒模样，黄昏时分走近过大瀑布，清晨散步时远眺过黄果树。有一次，安顺市电视台现场采访我，甚至就以黄果树大瀑布作的后景，我时常对远道而来的朋友说，观赏大瀑布，有多个角度，可以自上而下看，也可以自下而上仰望，更可以左看、右看、前看、后看。这样，才能真正领略大瀑布的风貌和神采。今天修筑的这一条游客栈道，就是顺着古时驿道的走势，为所有客人提供多滩观赏、感悟大瀑布的移动场所。一路走来，过罗洪桥（《徐霞客游记》中的白虹桥）、美军抗战浮雕、霞客亭，不知不觉间，就到了挑水河边。

白水河的这一段，之所以被称为挑水河，是因为古时两岸的苗族、布依族百姓，天天到这里来挑水饮用。水质清冽澄亮，喝来甘甜爽口。挑水河的下游一侧，便是洗衣河。是少数民族妇女洗衣裳的地方。"男挑水来女洗衣"，互不干扰，互相不到对方的区域去。正是受此启发，我小说中虚构了"太阳湾""月亮潭"的地名。

走过挑水河栈道，便是风雨长廊了，游客在此小憩时，就能看到右边的榕树园区。最早听说黄果树由黄葛树演变而来的典故，就是这附近村寨上的老人告诉我的。

在挨近观赏黄果树大瀑布之前，有一座哥特式的石砌尖顶小教堂，建成于1898年，有一百多年的历史了，不可不看。前面我多次提及的半边街，是抗日战争中著名的史迪威公路的必经之路，抗战中美军的运输兵到达黄果树之后，必须在这里修整。一是观赏黄果树大瀑布放松心情；二是进小教堂做心灵的洗礼；三是再往前走就要过"二十四道拐"的险峻地势了，那可是日军飞机重点轰炸的地方，得确认安全、道路畅通才能前行。栈道旁建有美军抗战浮雕，就是为了纪念这一段历史。

让我惊喜不绝的是,来到黄果树大瀑布跟前,自上而下俯视,我看到了七色彩虹,在犀牛潭山涧之间迎着雪浪般的瀑布飞涛而横跨,一道一道又一道,竟然是整整三条!

游客们雀跃欢呼,纷纷拿起手机、相机、摄影机拍摄留念,要留下这一珍贵的瞬间。

我也笑了。

是啊,几十次来过黄果树,我还是第一次看见三条彩虹为大瀑布系上锦带。

我情不自禁地写下了这首小诗。回到上海以后,细细回味,仍然意犹未尽,遂欣然写下了这一篇《黄果树的歌》。

读者朋友,你不觉得,该为黄果树唱一首歌了吗?

情在贵州山水间

黄果树瀑布

# 黄果树的彩虹

去过黄果树大瀑布好多次。从年轻时坐着卡车路过，在公路上眺望大瀑布，到成了作家，应邀细游大瀑布；从陪着到大瀑布来游览的客人观大瀑布，到在大瀑布旁的旅馆里过夜；从一个一个详尽地游览大瀑布群落的每一挂瀑布，到大瀑布周边的景点；从冬游瀑布，到春夏游瀑布；从大雨中的瀑布，到细雨中的瀑布；从夜间看彩灯瀑布，到晨起望雾中的瀑布……可以说，黄果树大瀑布的各种景观，我看了一个够。

但是，唯一的遗憾，就是从来没有看见过黄果树大瀑布的彩虹。看见过黄果树彩虹的游客，回来后形容起那景色时眉飞色舞的神情，逗得我心子痒痒的，好一阵羡慕。黄果树管理局的朋友告诉我，你要看黄果树大瀑布的彩虹，是要有几个先决条件的。

我问：啥子条件？其一，天气要好，要选出太阳的日子。我连忙说出大太阳的日子我都去过几次，从来碰不到。光是出太阳还不够，还得是水雾多的时间。水雾我也见过多次，太阳照在水雾上，只见水雾蒸腾，看不见彩虹。我连连摇头。还有一个条件是观察的角度。在人的视角和太阳光照折射的角度成 45°时，彩虹就显现出来了……

哎呀呀，这么复杂啊！怪不得我去过那么多次，都没见过彩虹呢！介绍的朋友仍在继续喋喋不休地宣传：要选在秋天，早上九点前后，太阳光从东南那侧照到大瀑布时，人站在水帘洞第三、第四、第五个窗洞往对岸和犀牛潭看，就会看见双彩虹。你多待一会，彩虹会随着阳光上升，会看到对面象鼻岭看台上的游客们，仿佛恰好在彩虹顶上。

我伸了伸舌头，完了，这么多苛刻、讲究的条件我是没福分看到黄果树的彩虹了。不过心底深处，我又不服气。去澳大利亚访问，游览英国女王盛赞过的"世界最美的地方"岚山时，我在雨后还见过彩虹呢！澳洲朋友都说我有运气。

贵州举办全国书展那一年,还没立秋,我陪上海文艺出版社的社长游黄果树。那天一大早从贵阳出发,不到九点就进入了焕然一新的景区,晨雾尚未散尽,游客也还不多,未到大瀑布跟前,哈,我们看见了什么?

    除了雾浪纷飞的大瀑布,悬在雪白的瀑布跟前的,显然是绚丽的彩虹!犀牛潭侧边斜斜的一条成弧形弯到山崖上;旁边稍低处又是一条,它似乎在尽力伸展腰肢,费劲地把大瀑布拴住。最长最美最为神奇的一条是悬在大瀑布中间的彩虹,太阳光斜斜地照射过来,让它焕发出炫目的色彩。游客们兴奋地纷纷朝着彩虹挥手、欢呼,又喊又叫,争相以它为背景拍照,仿佛黄果树的彩虹是大家的一位久违的朋友。

    我站在那里,心里忖度着:哦,黄果树的彩虹,我终于看见你了。

赤水丹霞十丈洞大瀑布

# 双挂大瀑布

贵州的瀑布很多，但是最有名的大瀑布，就是两处：黄果树大瀑布和赤水大瀑布。

赤水大瀑布原先叫十丈洞大瀑布，知名度比黄果树大瀑布略逊色一些。

为什么呢？

很多人看到赤水大瀑布的照片，会脱口而出，这是黄果树大瀑布。

不怪这些外省人，两挂大瀑布，确实有相像之处。不细看，还真容易搞错。黄果树大瀑布宣传得早，而且编进过课文，离公路也近，离贵州的两座大城市贵阳和安顺，都要比赤水大瀑布近得多，故而它的知名度大。

人们一讲起贵州，同时就会讲到黄果树大瀑布，就像讲到遵义会议和茅台酒一样自然。

而赤水大瀑布呢，宣传得稍微晚了一点，又改过名字。故而它的知名度就稍见逊色。而且还有一个原因，很多人看

过赤水大瀑布的游客,回来以后说,赤水大瀑布和黄果树大瀑布差不多。既然差不多,很多看过黄果树大瀑布的客人,就不想再去看赤水的瀑布了。况且赤水那么远,离四川都很近了,费那么多脚力和时间干啥子?

  这是游客心理。

  我这篇小文之所以把两挂大瀑布放在一起写,就是想说,赤水大瀑布和黄果树大瀑布除了相似之处,还有许多不同之处。

赤水四洞沟瀑布群

我们要强调的,就是它们之间的不同之处。比如说赤水大瀑布所处的丹霞地貌;比如去看赤水大瀑布,还能看到别处见不着的桫椤、竹海景观;比如赤水大瀑布所在的赤水河大峡谷两岸,还有独特的风情,它的峡谷景观,一点儿也不比科罗拉多大峡谷逊色。我们的赤水河是淌酒的河,淌出的都是赫赫有名的美酒,美国的科罗拉多大峡谷,淌得出酒来么?

除了强调赤水大瀑布和黄果树大瀑布的不同之处,我还要建议和呼吁搞一个"双挂瀑布游"的活动,就是游大瀑布、赏大瀑布、领略大瀑布的风姿与雄奇。

届时,黄果树大瀑布可以率整个黄果树的瀑布群落,以观水为主;赤水大瀑布则以断崖嶂谷、色若沃丹的丹霞地貌为主,让人们对双挂大瀑布留下难以忘怀的印象。

"双挂瀑布游"是需要眼界和胸怀的,无论是黄果树瀑布景区,还是赤水大瀑布景区,都需要有敞开的胸怀,有创新的视野,才能做好这一有创意的活动。

有人会说,从镇宁到赤水,那么远,搞得成吗?

有人会讲，我看到一处，以后再抽时间去看另一处，不行吗？

我要说，效果和感觉是不一样的。旅游就该有新的点子，新的创举。

想一想，当一次旅行就能看到两挂在中国乃至亚洲数一数二的大瀑布，当双挂瀑布同时出现在我们的手机中，贵州的旅游就会给人创新的思路和感受。

# 黄果树协奏曲

从 19 岁时去贵州插队当知青，和地处西南的贵州山乡结缘有 55 年了。半个多世纪以来，从当年知青时代搭上加了篷子的卡车去游览黄果树，花去了搭车费一元四角钱；直到去年的秋末到果树开会，在黄果树宾馆小住了几天，我都记不清自己多少次游览过黄果树了，雨天里来过，夏日里到过，晴好的天气里住过，并以不同的角度欣赏过大瀑布的美景。从第一次站在卡车旁久久地观赏黄果树大瀑布开始，我就觉得耳畔有奏鸣曲响起，节奏感非常强烈。直到去年秋天，夜深人静了，我提议去看大瀑布夜景，同行的伙伴虽然不解，但听了我的建议，还是去看了。到了夜色里的黄果树大瀑布观景台前，所有的人都不由自主安静下来，居高临下地瞅着远远地那一挂大瀑布。我分明又感觉到了黄果树的奏鸣曲，既有层次感，又无限的壮美和悠长。

在上海和各地的报刊上，我发表过几篇和黄果树有关的文章。记得第一篇是《黄果树瀑布群落》，介绍的是黄果树并非人们惯常见过的那一挂大瀑布,而是整整一个瀑布群落,足有十七、八幅之多。并挑选落差最大的关岭大瀑布,跌泻十八级的那大关瀑布,瀑顶最宽的陡坡塘瀑布以及银链坠潭瀑布等等逐一地写了写。

目的就是告诉游客朋友们,好不容易到了黄果树,不要只看了一挂瀑布,把其他的美景错过了。

后来我又写过难得一见的《黄果树的彩虹》,写过景区焕然一新的《黄果树的歌》,在文中写到黄果树瀑布为什么没有黄果?黄果树瀑布的遗憾,黄果树瀑布是贵州第一美景,名声也最大,为什么偏偏没有评上世界自然遗产?而其他景点,却一申请就被评上了。

从去年秋天在黄果树晚秋的季节里开会回来,我就想要写这一篇萌动在心的黄果树奏鸣曲了。

白天和夜晚站在大瀑布跟前,我看到的是当地布依族老乡平时经常讲到的平水期的景观。也就是最常见、最普通的景色。这个时候,大瀑布明显地分为四支,秀美而各显姿色,各有形态,从左侧至右边,第一支瀑布水势最小,相比较而言也单薄一些。但正因这一点,这一支瀑布呈现股潇洒的秀美之姿,洒脱而又自如地撒得很开。第二支瀑布就显出雄壮的气势,也是想整个黄果树瀑布的核心主力,水势大不说,自上而下倾吐般坠落,令人震撼,豪壮无比。第三支瀑布对比第二支,其大瀑布的气势略显逊色,和上下一般雄壮奔泻下来的第二支瀑布不同,第三支是上大下小,让人会产生疑惑,上头那么大一股飞瀑,为啥落进潭里之前,会一下子收窄了。其他水飞溅到哪里去了?顺便提前说一句,大瀑布后面的水帘洞,就是这么被发现的。40多年前,电视连续剧《西游记》中的水帘洞一景,就是在这里拍摄的。第三支瀑自上而下飞坠到水帘同前,一半的水势全涌往洞口而来。我陪同客人游览黄果树大瀑布,只要时间允许,我总会在充分观赏了大瀑布景色之后,领着客人旁边拐口的山道走上去,绕到大瀑布后面,从水帘洞前走过。当然,事前得备好雨具,走过水帘洞前面时,淋一点瀑布水,那是免不了的。但这种体验的乐趣和妙处在于,是一种独特的感受。想想嘛,我们一辈子走南闯北,游历无数高山大川,远近观赏过多少的瀑布景观。请问:

什么时候我们站到过一挂瀑布后面?

况且,真站到瀑布后头,稳住神,拂去满脸的水沫,透过喧嚣热烈的大水帘,能看到瀑布前方远近山坡和观景台前无数游人在向着黄果树眺望。

穿过水帘洞,哪怕只一次,也会成为每位游客终生难忘的记忆。

只因与贵州结缘了55年,我无数次地游览过黄果树。

不仅充分细致地观赏过黄果树雄奇的平水期景观。枯水时节，因天旱而多日无雨，上游的打邦河、白水河来水减少、减弱，黄果树瀑布的水势只剩下一大片薄薄的水帘，垂挂在那里，连平时喧腾的水声也减弱到勉强能辨别的地步。每当这时候，我就觉得奏鸣曲进入了低谷，但那分明仍显示出瀑布难得一见的美。而那旋律，也自有一股韵味。

而更多的时候，多雾多雨的贵州，黄果树的上游，总能保证充沛的雨量和来水。特别是到了雨季，大瀑布的气势之雄壮豪迈，是难以用语言来描述和形容的。

那年的春夏之交，黄果树上游的大山里暴发了山洪。我恰好路过景区，刚去到门口，就听到从来没听见过的阵阵轰隆之声。管理区主任告诉我，瀑布变成了一头巨龙，水色泛黄，看过去就是直冲而来的一条大河，暴怒了一般，已经不对游客开放。不过，观测水文、水势的平台上还是安全的，我可以陪同你去看看。

我怎会错过这千载难逢的机会，随着管委会几个人一齐走上水文平台。哇，那大瀑布像整条河流崩塌了一般汹涌澎湃得像狂怒的黄龙往何河谷里直冲而去，那狂野的怒浪发出震天动地的巨吼。我们互相之间说什么话都听不见，只能靠眼神和手势表达我们的惊讶和震撼。

这真的是难逢难遇的黄果树。

但星,在大多数日子里,黄果树大瀑布都是令人赏心悦目的。秋天是秋日里的美景,春天有春日的浪漫。走进景区,无论远眺还是走近犀牛潭前,都会别有一番风韵和感受,看雾岚、观水色、听瀑声,都能觉得大瀑布在奏喧着一首不息的生命之歌,蓬勃欢畅的歌。

哦,正如明朝时期徐霞客见到的黄果树瀑布是这般模样,今天成千上万的人看到的黄果树大瀑布,还是这般模样。相信,多少年之后,黄果树大瀑仍会以它的雄姿秀色,屹立在云贵高原上。这是不是从另一个侧面,也印证了这么一个道理:

山水是主人,我们只是过客。

扫码跟随
叶辛游贵州

黄果树瀑布
荔波小七孔
西江千户苗寨
赤水丹霞
兴义万峰林
铜仁梵净山

荔波小七孔卧龙潭瀑布

# 神曲小七孔

在《爱上荔波》这本书中,我写过一篇《小七孔的喧》。为什么还要写小七孔是神曲呢?

只因这是我在小七孔一段难忘的记忆。

写小七孔的喧声,主要是描绘小七孔桥下的响水河,日夜带给居住在附近的布依、水、苗、瑶各族老乡和今天蜂拥而来的游客们的感觉。清澄如碧的响水河给人的美景。

而称呼小七孔是神曲,具有小夜曲般的悠远和陶醉的美,则是我在黎明时分坐在小七孔边上时独特的感受。

一般的游客,到了世界遗产地,面对一个又一个令人流连忘返的景点,只能无奈地带着赶时间的遗憾,匆促忙乱地赶路,生怕漏下了啥精彩的景点没有见到,也没有留下镜头。

即使在景点附近民宿入住下来的客人,赶早起来后,也不可能找着交通工具在拂晓时分来到小七孔桥边。

而我,早就是荔波各族老乡的朋友了,和这块土地结缘了半个世纪。头天夜里和一个文人说好,他乐呵呵地笑道:

"叶老师，一言为定，明天一大早，我陪着你悄悄地到小七孔去，感受一下天蒙蒙亮时候的小七孔。我有车。"

朋友是个水族知识分子，虽也是文人，却仍不改他那率直爽朗的个性，对我补充道：

"就我们俩去，我一个伙伴也不喊。"

没想到他说的一大早，竟然是天还没亮呢。

我正在熟睡中，他那辆小车就在我楼下鸣了两声短促的喇叭。

当我坐上他车时，他一边发动车子，一边道："我们悄悄地进去，打枪的不要。从这里开往景区，还得二十几分钟哩！"

果然，车子从山路上直插过去，开到景区门前平时售票的地方时，售票厅、检票口都还没开哩。水族朋友道：

"他们还没到上班时候呢！我们可以直接进去。"

下车移开了挡道的路障，他还不无乖张地做了一个鬼脸。"出来的时候，我们补票也不迟。县里面给我开了路条，你放心，我们不犯规。"

其实景区领导我也认识，是个刚毕业不久的大学生，是这边瑶区培养的第一个瑶族女大学生，上大学时，听过我的课。

我们下车来到小七孔桥时，我从睡梦中被喊醒的倦意顿时一扫而光。

天哪！这是我多次在白天里见过的小七孔景区吗？

只见在拂晓时分朦朦胧胧的晨色里，桥孔、桥身覆盖着浓密绿荫的"小七孔"宛如仙境，响水河面上凝然不动地浮动着白色的雾纱，小七孔桥时隐时现地似在黎明的晓色中穿行。它似乎也有着灵性般从夜的沉睡中苏醒过来。

水族汉子从车子上拿下了摄影器材，一改他那耿直的性格，放低声音对我说：

"叶老师，你随意感受，我也要工作了。"

说着，走一旁去选择角度架设他的机器了。

我选中一块不大不小的山石，手一摸，有露水，我掏出几张餐巾纸抹拭了几下，将就平顺的山石坐了下来。

从小七孔桥两侧的山坡树林里传出一声两声雀儿的啼鸣。

天渐渐亮了，眼前的山色、景物尤其是小七孔桥清晰起来。

我置身于这山野的幽深宁静之中，只有响水河流淌的声音和早醒鸟儿的鸣声。

我真正地感受到了自然界中"溪声喧亦静"的神妙境界。

噢，我的身畔分明响起了小夜曲的鸣奏声，悠扬、醉然得如诗如梦。不、不、不！不是一般的小夜曲，而是神曲。

我双手抱膝，坐在石头上，从身心里涌出的神曲似在由一支无形的乐队演奏。不知为什么，响水河的流水，当下显得出奇地平顺，水面平静、水色如玉，涂抹着一层层绿色的两岸山岭，恰似一幅巨大的浓郁油画。整个小七孔景区，在我的眼前像煞一只巨型的盆景。噢，小七孔的美是立体的，那绿色的层次远近高低都不同。小七孔的美是实实在在的，我本人就置身其中，伸手就可以触摸到身边的石头、石块、苔藓和河里的水。小七孔的美也是如诗如画的，都说最美的山水画得留白，待在小七孔桥畔，连留白处也让人觉得美不胜收。

天色亮堂起来了，不过太阳的光还没有越过周边高耸秀丽的山峰，小七孔景区的所有色彩都明亮起来了。

我感觉这首神曲，也仿佛在指挥棒无形的挥动之下激越、欢快、喜悦起来。

不是么，放眼望去，远处响水河的68级跌水瀑布群像一条摇摇晃晃、腾跃跳荡的银链般，不息地舞动着。

全世界的瀑布都是从山崖间飞泻而下、直坠河谷的。唯独这68级瀑布群，是顺着河谷自高而低躺在溪流中奔腾下来。不知有多少游客在不知不觉间走到了瀑布尽头，又折返回来道："我真不舍得离开这么美的地方，真舍不得！"

每当我听到中外游客对我说出这句话，我就会提醒他对他道："你感觉神曲在演奏么……"

# 小七孔的喧

小七孔就是一座桥,一头连接着广西,一头通贵州。它架在涵碧潭上,因有七个桥孔而被简称为"小七孔"。

小七孔传得远近闻名,使得人们将其原来的名字"万古兴桥"都忘记了。

有人提醒我,说小七孔是在峡谷里僻静处的一座桥,并不喧哗。

不等我反应过来,便有人反驳说,怎么不喧嚣,你听听,桥下响水河的流水,日夜都在欢腾着奔流。无人的时候,响水河的声音,才响亮呢!

是啊,响水河、响水河,就是响的嘛!再说了,今天讲的小七孔,已经不是仅仅只指这一座建于清朝道光年间的古桥,而是指的整个小七孔景区了。

不少外省人,时常连荔波其他的景点都记不住,只记住了一个小七孔。

不是吗,宣传荔波的画册、书籍、报刊、名片上,印的都是小七孔。连荔波的文学杂志,干脆也叫小七孔。难得来

俯瞰小七孔喀斯特峰林地貌

一回的外方人,自然就只记得:世界遗产地,是小七孔了。

有人说小七孔是绿绒绣出来的,绿得深沉幽然,令人流连忘返。

有人说小七孔是翠染的,真正的一块大自然的翠玉啊!

还有人说小七孔是一首诗,是一幅让人忘不了的油画、是一支时常萦绕在心头的歌。

我说小七孔岂止是一首诗啊,一批批的文人墨客来了又

去,他们为小七孔写下了多少首诗、多少篇赞颂的散文与随笔啊!

几次走进小七孔景区,来写生的画家、来拍照片的摄影师,为小七孔拍下的照、画出的风景,可以成千上万来计了吧。

还有不少歌词作者和歌唱家,不止一次地为小七孔歌咏,为小七孔陶醉了吧。

小七孔是写不完、画不完、唱不完的。一百好几十年了,黔桂道上,世间的人来来往往,来了又去,小七孔仍在吸引着一拨又一拨的海内外客人前来。

除了景色诱人,小七孔究竟还有啥吸引我们的地方?

在离涵碧潭水面四米多高的这座古桥上,我来回走过;在清晨林间的鸟语声中,小七孔桥畔静寂无人的环境里,我坐在石头上沉思过;在游人如织,姑娘们欢叫着高举双手在桥面上留影时,听着她们的笑语,我也想过。

到了这儿,人们的情绪为什么会不由自主的亢奋起来,高涨起来,是什么吸引着操各种语言的游客们蜂拥而来?

我是在荔波的洪村认识何秀娟的,我问她:"在小七孔成为景区之前,从洪村到小七孔那边去,很远吧?"

她说:"不短。"

我又问道:"那么,在你小时候,小七孔还不是旅游点时,你去过那里吗?"

她笑了,说:"叶老师,我就是小七孔附近的村寨上长大的,小时候经常去小七孔玩。可欢呢!"

我知道问对人了,何秀娟是布依族,她的回答同时告诉我,小七孔周边团转,不但有瑶寨,还有布依寨。我就请她讲下去。

她说:"当小姑娘时,她也要帮着家里掏猪草、放牛,只要一来到小七孔桥周围,一帮娃娃就会放下背篼和小刀,在小七孔桥上、桥边疯玩,也不晓得是咋个回事,就觉得好玩,玩得快活又尽兴。有时候,她还会坐上爸爸的捕鱼船,顺着响水河到大七孔那边去捕鱼。"

我脑子里想象得出她所说的画面,并由此得出一个结论:人来到了风景秀美的地方,哪怕是小孩子,也会情不自禁地受到风光景物的影响,兴奋起来,高兴起来,玩得疯起来。

还有人说小七孔是一个梦,进入了她的梦境里,人会腾云驾雾,想入非非,会在亦真亦幻中进入一个神奇的境界。那时候,小七孔不是一座桥,而是勾人魂魄的山水,它和葱茏蓊郁的峰峦,和映出人脸的涵碧潭水相依相融,只能用"美梦"二字才能形容出那种感觉。从美梦中醒过来,人还会有种心醉的陶然。

徜徉在小七孔桥上,我从荔波这一头眺望过对岸的广西地域,然后又跨过25米的桥面,从广西那边回望过荔波的山野。两地都是绿林密布的山山岭岭,两岸的山岭同样的滋润浓翠,翠绿把一座七孔的人造桥梁几乎都掩盖了。有时候我会突发奇想,在1836年之前,还没有造起小七孔桥的时候,这个幽静的峡谷是什么样子呢?住在附近村寨上的瑶族、布依族老乡,来到涵碧潭前,如何相对眺望呢?

没有人对我的想法感兴趣,现存的《荔波县志稿》中也无记载,相似的荔波八景中,同样无记载。

离开小七孔桥5公里处,还有一座大七孔桥,比小七孔桥晚建成15年。当地村民称这两座桥是姊妹桥。近40年前,我初次听说茂兰和大小七孔时,无论是村寨上的老百姓,还是荔波县、黔南州里的干部,都用赞不绝口的语气,把这地方称作是"仙境"般美的所在,是"神仙"居住的环境。

到了今天,这只有神仙才有福气待的如诗如画的景,已经来到了我们身边。

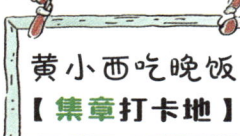

黄果树瀑布
荔波小七孔
西江千户苗寨
赤水丹霞
兴义万峰林
铜仁梵净山

扫码跟随
叶辛游贵州

情在贵州山水间

# 弦歌四季的西江

写过一篇《西江华彩路》,《人民日报》登了;隔开一个月,《贵州日报》又以一个整版的篇幅,配了几张他们报社记者照下的彩色照片,转载了这篇小文。

省里读者读了,说我写得到位。

县里的读者读了,说叶老师你再来我们这里,我们请您吃道地的苗族菜肴,喝米酒。

州里有领导对我说,文化人就是文化人,你看我时常陪方方面面的客人去西江,都写不出这样的文章。

其实写《西江华彩路》,我是在一个苗族小伙的陪伴之下,悄悄去的。苗族小伙子是西江人,我跟他约法三章,不要给旅游公司的领导说我去了,不要给县里的方方面面说我去了,只要他一个人陪着我,我去哪里他走到哪里,陪我一起吃饭,晚上给我找个民宿,一般的就行。

我这篇《西江华彩路》,就是在苗族小伙小杨一整天一晚上的陪伴之下完成的。为了核实西江苗寨的居民户数和老少百姓共计多少人，我们一起走进了村委会，查看了具体的户籍。

回到上海之后，我根据这两天26个小时的采访和感受，写下了这篇文章。

当然不是说我采访的效率高，也不是能写。我和西江苗寨结缘半个世纪了，曾经无数次地来过这里。

不仅看到了西江苗寨的今天，而且知道西江苗寨的昨天、前天，十几年前、五十多年前的西江是什么模样，都还留在我的记忆深处。

是在长期感受的基础上，我才把《西江华彩路》写出来的。

比如说"西江"这两个字，在苗语中是"美女"的意思，很多游玩过西江的客人就不知道。

我自以为这篇文章写得还可以，县里有领导碰到我，还夸耀说：

"叶老师，你这篇文章，上了《人民日报》，又登《贵州日报》，比我们往常请好多人，编一本书的效果还要好！"

我听了都喜滋滋的。

哪晓得，文章影响大了，离西江很近的朗德苗寨对我有意见了。他们对我说："叶老师，你年轻的时候就来过朗德，我们还留着你来时照的相呢，你怎么不写写我们朗德呢？我们朗德的变化同样很大，旅游客人来得也多啊！"

西江苗寨敬酒习俗『高山流水』

我只得赔笑脸,无言可答。为啥呢?他们说的是大实话。

其实,不仅仅朗德苗寨,属于黔东南的很多苗寨,我都去过。比如苗家短裙民俗村新桥,比如芦笙之村排卡,谢寨风雨桥,铜鼓村的苗族农民画,苗家温泉村……都是旅游的好景点,都是颇具特色的民族村寨。但是,我们实事求是地说一句,西江苗寨,是最为突出、最热闹,外来客人去得最多的苗家村落。

春、夏、秋、冬四季,西江苗寨天天都是欢声笑语、歌舞不绝、人流如潮,这样的盛况,即使拿到全世界面前,都是有一比的。法国巴黎也是游客如潮的地方,巴黎圣母院、

45

卢浮宫，走进去参观得排队，我也曾一一去游过，但是其人流和热闹劲儿，和西江苗寨无法比。前几年的夏天，我在贵阳街上碰到西江苗寨上的一位中学教师，他告诉我，西江苗寨上天天喧声如潮，旅游客人超过了二三万人。如果你要下来，一定得事先通知我们，要不然，吃饭你都吃不上，夜晚的宿处都难找。

是啊，作为一个典型的苗族村寨，西江确实是一个个案。成功范例的个案。

要认识今天的西江苗寨，得从历史的角度去了解和思考。

要懂得今天的西江苗寨，得从民族风情的特点去分析和观察。

要理解今天的西江苗寨，得走进黔东南的苗寨侗村布依人家，住下来和村民们好好地聊天摆谈，听听他们说些什么，从他们由衷的言谈中和唱出的古歌里，读懂他们的心声。

我十多次地走进西江苗寨，前后历经了半个多世纪。记得50多年前的1970年，我走进西江苗寨时，那种贫穷、闭塞和偏远，在我的心头激起的简直是震撼。

当我在上世纪80年代，以青年作家采风的名义走进西江苗寨时，村寨上的清净、寂寥和冷落，同样让我困惑：怎么只剩下老人和娃崽了呢？青壮年们去哪儿了？

答曰：思想大解放，不但青壮年男子汉们出去打工了，连姑娘和年轻媳妇们也跑去广东、广西、贵阳、重庆打工了。他们说外面世界里的票子好赚啊!

我听得目瞪口呆。

也可能正是有了整整一代人的外出闯荡吧,他们感受过了外面的世界,体验过了都市里的繁华和喧嚣,品尝过了城市里的饮食,他们意识到了苗寨生活的可贵和特点,他们把从外面世界里学到的东西,不知不觉地融进西江苗寨的生活形态之中。他们把防火意识贯穿到西江苗寨纯木楼的意识中,他们在突出饮食中苗家风味的同时,吸引进当代的饮食时尚……规划环境是这样,引导游客是这样,于是乎,几乎家家户户外出打工的西江人都回来了,他们在自己家门口接待全省、全国、全世界涌来的客人都忙不完,他们怎么还抽得出时间外出打工呢?

哦,弦歌四季的西江,其发展的当代历史,就是一首歌啊!

银装穿在身 巡游庆苗年

# 西江华彩路

西江苗寨,巍巍雄奇苗岭上空一颗闪烁光芒的星星。

西江苗寨,郁郁葱葱的雷公山白水河畔的一颗明珠。

半个世纪以来,西江苗寨和我结下了一生的情缘。

2018年的初夏时节,一个阳光明媚的日子,我又一次走进了西江苗寨。

这是我熟悉的西江苗寨吗?这是我无数次走进过的西江苗寨吗?是的是的,偌大的敢称世界干栏式建筑地标的一千四百七十二幢苗家木楼,仍然鳞次栉比地呈巨大的牛角状气势雄伟地坐落在东山坡上,路仍然是石板铺砌成的,那浓郁的飘散着酸香气息的苗家风味,仍然久久地弥散在空气之中。只是,只是我为啥感觉有点陌生了呢?只是我为啥还是感觉新奇、新鲜和那么点诧异呢?

于是我决定住下来,像年轻的时候在苗寨上住进老乡家中一样,在西江苗寨住上一晚。至少感受一下西江苗寨的白天和夜晚、黄昏和清晨,感受一下西江苗寨今天的二十四小时。正像苗歌里唱的：住在哪里都一样，哪里都是好家乡。好美的家乡。

### 青石古街

西江苗寨，很多到过这里的贵州人，都以为这是一个村寨。其实不然，这里有四个自然村寨，分别为羊排、东引、平寨、南贵。（注：这是今天按行政区划分的。当年，自然村落共有八个，现在已然连成了一片。）以往数次来这里，问到省有关部门的人，问到州里和县里干部，他们都会有把握地告诉我，西江苗寨共有一千二百户人家，每家一幢苗家木楼，所有的游客看到的顺坡而上建到东山坡高处的典型苗家干栏式木楼，共有一千二百多幢。

这一次我走进村委会，查验了户籍，西江苗寨共有一千四百七十二户，共计五千六百六十八人。苗家木楼的总数在一千五百幢上下。

不过，据说，西江苗寨上常年居住着七八千人。

今年四十五岁的莫世海告诉我，"光是我任总经理的'西江千户苗寨文化旅游公司'旗下，雷山县旁边的剑河、凯里、黄平几个县来就业、打工的，就有七百多人。叶老师，你想一想，西江苗寨上今年已达三百八十家的饭店、酒家、农家

乐，也都雇得有人，加起来只怕七八千还不止！"

这真的是西江苗寨发展旅游之后的新气象。记得十几年之前，我也来采访过，那时候，西江苗寨上的中青年苗家，都涌到广东、浙江沿海一带去打工了。散落在西江几个村寨上的老人和娃崽，一遇到要干重一点的体力活，找不到一个青壮年。

现在是下午3点多钟，我信步走在青石和鹅卵石铺设的古街上。哎呀，古街上的人流堪比上海的南京路步行街。家家铺子里挤满了购买和观看民族服饰和工艺品的游客，街面上的人流潮水般地从这一头涌过来，从那一头淌过去，满耳里是悦耳的歌声，满眼里看到的是即兴的舞蹈。宽敞一点的地势，只要有人放声一唱，就聚起了人堆，真叫作是"八层人坐，十层人站"，吸引着远方来的游客们停下来观赏苗家风情浓郁的歌舞。电瓶车按响喇叭慢吞吞地在人潮之中前行，人们刚刚避开的过道旋即又被欢声笑语的人群填满。

有节奏的鼓声"砰咚砰咚"敲击着，所有人的目光不由被吸引地望去。原来是一帮苗族老汉和奶奶，他们两人一行并肩而行，排着长队，穿着统一的黑色苗族服饰，老奶奶佩戴着闪闪放光的银饰，老汉们则穿着苗族汉子的传统紧身衣衫，他们每人手中撑着一把油纸伞，随着鼓点的节奏，不疾不徐、不慌不忙地踩着鼓点前行。围观的游客们顿时察觉了这一支队伍独特的美，他们有的举起手中的相机，有的就用手机，拍摄下苗族老人们风姿绰约的舞步和形象，还有的游客干脆亮起嗓门，高声夸耀着：

"好！好一场独有的广场秀！"

从贵阳陪着我下西江的小杨，本身就是雷山县的苗族，不由对我说：

"西江的老人娃娃，个个都有事儿干。看嘛，这些老人，每天这个时辰，都到古街上走半个小时，活动了筋骨，也给古街增添了一道景观。天天都有人朝着他们叫好！比年轻的姑娘小伙跳的舞还要受欢迎！"

七十四岁的苗族老人宋国伦对我说："西江的娃娃们忙读书；老人们现在都有事儿干，有工作，有工资，参与分红……"

"分红？"我追着问，"分啥子红？"

"门票的百分之十八，拿来分给西江的每家每户。看你工作的多少，钱不少的呢！老人们的积极性高得很！"

小杨补充道："过去老人们在家忙种田，上雷公山砍柴，烧炭，现在这些活都不干了！"

"为啥？"我又问。

"忙不过来啊。"宋国伦老汉道。

"那么，农家的活谁来干呢？"我不由得问，"每天有八九千的游客涌进西江,都要吃农家饭菜,都要尝尝酸汤鱼,那么多的糯米饭和蔬菜,那么多的鱼,总要有人养殖和种出来呀!"

"鱼是剑河大水库里喂养的。"宋国伦老汉简短地说,"每天汽车运过来。"

"粮食和蔬菜,"小杨接着道,"也是附近几个县供应过来的。要不怎么说,西江苗寨的游客,带动了周边几个县的经济呢!"

"我那旅游公司的七百多名农民工,除却剑河的,还有台江、黎平、施秉过来的。为啥雇那么多人呢?就是西江人忙不过来了呀!"莫世海说,"在西江,老的有老的事干,年轻的有年轻的事干;漂亮的有漂亮的事干,长相一般的有长相一般的事儿干。人人都活得很充实。"

雷山检察院的郭苏斌,平时喜欢摄影,这一次在西江苗寨碰到我,他对我道:

"叶老师,1982年,我在西江中学教书,放农忙假,要带着娃娃们到水田里干活。天没亮4点钟就起床,紧赶慢赶走到田头,天刚刚亮,你想想这段路有多长。"

他这话给我留下很深的印象。西江苗寨这地方,是紧挨着雷公山的最末一个苗寨,再往山下走,就要进入雷公山的原始森林了,不适宜搞种植业和养殖业。重视民族文化,发展旅游产业，西江苗寨找准了路子，走对了道。

熙来攘往的游客们像电影院散场般在古街上涌动，不绝于耳的欢声笑语造成了一阵阵鼎沸的气息。

### 苗寨之夜

我不是第一次领略西江苗寨夜色的美。

有几次，在西江吃过晚饭，我都是等到夜幕降临，登上观景台，把繁星点点的万家灯火看个够，这才离去，回凯里或是贵阳下榻。除了年轻时代在苗寨的阁楼上居住，我都没在西江苗寨的旅舍里过夜。

这一回不同，我入住的农家乐位置比景观台还要高，还要佳。

白天，喝着茶，我已经将西江苗寨的全景来来回回看了几遍。人们说，到西江苗寨来旅游，看什么？

我说看风景、看风情、看风光。

东山坡两座山峰，犹如两只巨大的突兀而起的水牛角。西江苗族的祖先，视牛为神圣物的老祖公们，仿佛受到沟通祖辈灵魂的点拨和启示，要求世世代代的西江苗族的后裔，随山就势地修村建寨。一代一代遵从祖训的苗家儿女，发挥他们的聪明才智，巧夺天工，经千百年来几十代人的努力，建成了今天呈现在我们面前的中国独有、世界无双、气势磅礴的苗族大寨。

如果说，白天我在露台上把整个苗族的穿枋吊脚楼，把苗家的建筑文化、田园风光，把新型的旅游民族风情细细地观赏了的话，这会儿，坐在夜的露台上，更觉得灯火辉煌，霓虹璀璨的点点繁星，恰似造型奇美的仙阁琼楼，如同天上人间般的华丽，流水啊，绿树啊，古树木桥啊，吊脚木楼啊，全都交相辉映着，尤似苗族古歌中赞颂的童话世界。

我坐了很久，一直坐到旁边桌子上五六个北京游客离去，坐到两个中年女游客喁喁细语说尽了回客房，坐到角落那边的一对青年情侣打着哈欠离开，我仍然坐在那里，远眺着东山坡的美景出神。

苗家小姑娘来给我续水，我向她打听："这灯光每天亮到什么时候？"

她甜甜地笑着，用轻柔的语调告诉我，过了半夜，两三点钟的样子，灯光才会渐次熄灭。她像是提醒我道：

"西江苗寨常对客人们说，我们这里的西边山坡，每一处农家乐都是观景台；东边山坡呢，处处都是舞台。你听，《美丽西江》的歌舞剧，正演到尾声哩！"

西江苗寨正中央的表演场，苗家歌舞的欢笑声和时而激越、时而舒缓的放歌，我仍然能隐隐约约辨别出来的。我甚至能分得出哪是抒情的飞歌,哪是苍凉的叙述盘古开天地以来的古歌,哪是欢乐的节日庆典歌,哪是情意绵绵的男女对歌……一整个晚上,与其说我是坐在栏杆边出神,不如说我是在凝神倾听,是在随着歌声一会儿昂扬、一会儿低回而沉思默想。

我想到了当知青时住在苗寨的阁楼上,那真是穷得恼火。说得含蓄一点,是温饱没有得到解决;说得直率一点,那就是冬天得靠政府拨下寒衣寒被,才能把冬天对付过去。而年年青黄不接的五黄六月间,还得依赖政府拨下回销粮、救济粮,才能渡过难关。

即便到改革开放初期,温饱是解决了,苗族老乡还是坦率地对我说,饭是有得吃了,娃崽一年也能缝一件新衣衫了,我们还是又穷又酸呀,靠酸菜辣椒下饭,一年到头吃一回肉,喝上一趟酒。青壮年纷纷跑到外头的世界去打工,有客人来,拿点酸菜、苦薯酒就算迎客。你那些年来时,不是还说,我们苗乡侗寨山水自然风光美,人仍然穷,是富饶的贫困嘛!

那些年里,不止一个成了家的壮年汉子、青年小伙对我说过:"叶老师,到外头打工,是能赚到比家乡勤扒苦挣种田多的钱,可我们精神上也苦啊!过年回家乡,娃娃认不得亲爹。远在他乡,挨骂受训是不用说了,思念娃娃,想念婆娘,牵挂老人那种滋味,真是难熬啊!这种远离亲情的痛苦,我们喜欢歌、喜欢舞的苗家,更难忍受呀。"

我保存下来的采访笔记上,那些年里,西江苗寨到外省去打工的青壮年,占到百分之九十六到百分之九十八。

而现今,除了读书当上了教授、副教授的,进步快当上了干部的之外,西江苗寨所有的青壮年,都在家门口就业,过上了安定祥和、老少家人团聚、其乐融融的生活。

袁刚县长给了我一组数据,独特、丰厚、风情浓郁、历史悠久的苗族大地域文化,促进了西江苗寨的大旅游,这股井喷式的大旅游势头,促进了西江苗寨的大发展。而发展起来的西江苗寨,愈加珍惜家乡方方面面的文化资源。

我眺望着夜色里的西江苗寨全景,陡地感到,灯光闪耀之中层层叠叠、鳞次栉比、气势恢宏的吊脚木楼群,恍若一只振翅欲飞、凌空而起的银色巨蝶。哦,那是不是和苗族神话、古歌中吟唱的蝴蝶妈妈灵犀相通呢?

## 西江清晨

下半夜,雷公山巅上照常地打雷了。惊天动地的雷声把我从酣睡中震醒过来,恍恍惚惚之间,我只觉得千百根巨大的圆木从山上滚落下来一般,"轰隆隆隆"地不绝于耳。

清醒过来之后,我细细地像知青时代在苗寨上生活时一样，辨别着一阵一阵的雷声，这是滚山雷、这是闷雷、这是落地雷、这是炸雷……雷声震耳，睡不着了，我索性亮了灯，坐起身子，枕着雷公山谛听。脑子里不时地掠过下西江之前，在贵阳读到的几篇学术文章：《西江的文化拐点》《西江模式——值得研究的民族文化旅游发展模式》《"西江模式"引领贵州全域旅游新方向》《用旅游扶贫模式迎接千户苗寨5A景区的创建》……读的时候，只感觉到，西江苗寨这十年来的发展，已经引起学术界的关注，人们纷纷把它当作研究对象，当作一个现象。在游客数量剧增，苗家收入提高，生活得安定祥和，吃肉成了常事的今天，历来信奉有酒同喝、有肉同吃这种均质化价值取向的苗家儿女，最大的变化是什么呢？

对了，明天早上，我得问问他们！就盯着这一点问。

雷公山上的雷声，渐去渐远，轰响一个多小时之后，平息了。我熄灯入睡。

是叽喳啁啾的鸟语把我唤醒的，推开窗户，一大股雷公山原始森林的气息扑面而来。哦，那是甜美的、清新的、沁人肺腑的草香原木气息，那是市井喧嚣的城市的早晨呼吸不到的。

我深深地吸了几大口醉人的空气，情不自禁探出头去。

西江苗寨正在我的眼前苏醒过来。天哪，我仿佛不认识她了,下半夜的一场雷雨,把西江苗寨的妆容彻底地洗刷了一遍,山啊,水啊,吊脚木楼啊,田坝坡上啊,一座座风雨桥啊,就连田埂小路、苗寨上袅袅娜娜升腾而起的轻烟薄雾,都似乎被画笔涂抹过一般,格外地清丽、明晰而悦目;郁郁葱葱的雷公山的原始森林上空,乳白色的晨雾凝滞不动,而飘飘悠悠的林岚缭绕着浓翠欲滴的杉木,轻纱薄绫般幻化开来。

太阳从东坡后面无声地跃出云层,顿时把整个西江苗寨的山水河谷树林村寨镀上一片光华,而交汇融合在一起的雾色林岚,随之变幻着、升腾着把万千气象一一地在我视野里徐徐展开。

我贪婪地凝视着眼前的一切。这是任何大家都画不出的大自然的瑰丽景致。

这是苗岭的早晨,西江苗寨的早晨,面对着东边山坡苏醒活跃起来的舞台,我又一次醒悟道:生活在西江苗寨的苗家儿女,为什么对这方山水、对山水间的草木如此敬畏、如此珍惜,因为他们自古以来遵循万物有灵的生存法则。故而在听到我问的问题时,他们会用质朴的语言说出一番深奥的道理。

到外头打工回来的农家乐店主,三十七岁的侯艳江对我说:

"外头的农家乐店主,都信奉去适应游客的口味。西江苗寨不一样,我们是要让客人们来适应苗家的口味。酸汤鱼、牛肉、农家小炒、糯米饭、鼓藏肉,那都是我们的饮食特色,这是我们的美食文化。我们自觉地保护这种饮食文化,还要传承给子孙后代,不做历史的罪人。"

吃饭是这样,盖房子也是一样。在北京打工十五年回到家乡的毛雨,他的专业是搞文创设计,他自豪地说:

"西江苗寨的每一幢新盖的木楼,都要修成传统的吊脚楼的模样。在我们这里,绝不会出现钱多了盖洋别墅那种事儿。只因为,我们每个人都晓得,我是西江人。"

我是西江人,吃西江的饭,穿西江苗族的服饰,住苗家的木楼,就连喝酒唱歌也一样。

在西江,有一首喝米酒时必唱的歌,我年轻时就会跟着唱,那里面最出名的两句是:"你喜欢要唱,不喜欢也要唱……"

这是西江苗寨千百年来的酒文化,就如同他们的歌文化、舞文化、芦笙文化、银饰文化、建筑文化一样。

一个苗族老汉在风雨桥上由衷地对我道:"在我们这里,不但不能见钱眼开乱建房,随便拆自家的老房子也不行。寨邻们都晓得,一拆就是拆文化……"

村支书蒋仕杰今年四十七岁了,2008年之前,一直在

广东、深圳打工,看够了外头世界赚钱的门道,他对我道:

"西江苗寨,淳朴的景,就是文化。现在这是大家的共识。我们西江的旅游得以发展,就一条,人文旅游,民族文化人文旅游。全省那么多旅游的地方,西江苗寨来的游客仅次于黄果树大瀑布,排名第二,靠的就是文化。"

我想,这就是西江苗寨和我当知青时不同的最大的变化吧。

太阳升上了雷公山高高的主峰山巅,把灿烂辉煌的万道霞光挥洒到苗岭的座座山头上,挥洒到西江苗寨的山水土地上,挥洒在这一片苗家的乐土上。

西江苗族妇女吹奏芦笙

# 烟雨西江

　　这里是西江苗寨的最高处,位于最佳观景平台旁的观察哨。透过玻璃望出去,西江苗寨两座酷似巨型水牛角的山坡上,繁星点点,全都在雨雾中闪烁着难得一见的美。这美是幻影似的,朦朦胧胧的,黔东南春夏之交的雨,落了整整一天了。这使得游客们感觉到一切都是湿漉漉的。可是,尽管碰到了雨季,却丝毫没有影响人们的热情。相反,观察哨门外的观景平台上,站满了摩肩接踵的游客。他们争相眺望着远方高低错落的景致,逗留的时间比平时还要长。我透过观察哨的大玻璃,远远地望去,一整个西江峡谷,全是喧嚣的声浪,鼎沸的欢声笑语,从透气孔里传进哨所中来。我凝神望去,撑着伞的,穿着雨衣的,戴着雨帽的,本身也都成了西江之夜一道特殊的风景。和6年前的初夏时节那个晴朗的夜晚相比,我只觉得,璀璨的灯光更亮了。尤其是那一条主街上,更是亮得耀眼,亮得令人惊叹。只见光影、光柱、光斑、光点的腾跃闪耀在我的眼前织成了一片光的世界,闪闪烁烁，五光十色。雷公山下雾了，雾影在霓虹灯般的光帘背景上，飘悠着，浮动着，浓浓的地方像云朵，而雾纱则像仙女般飘飘然地在山峦之间晃悠晃悠。哦，这是任何彩笔画不出来的巨幅作品，这是大自然的鬼斧神工赐给人间的烟雨西江梦幻美景。此时此刻，恍惚之间，我不觉得这是一个村寨，而是烟雨西江的一座山城。

世上独一无二的山城，有着现实美和梦幻美交织在一起的山城。

我们久久地眺望着这一派难得遇见的雨夜西江的奇景。四位观察员在雨夜里是最为放松的，他们平时最主要的任务是在晴朗的日子里瞭望火情，什么角落冒出了烟雾，什么地方燃起了异常的火光，及时地报告给随时准备出发的消防队员。在雨日里，无论是白天还是夜晚，火情是极少见的。但是他们仍然从不同的角度，观察着西江苗寨上东南西北山上山下乃至白水河畔的动静。

不怕一万，就怕万一啊。

傍晚的擦黑时分，我们走进西江苗寨的时候，陪同我们的县政协李胜平副主席告诉我，今天尽管落了一整天的雨，雨势时大时小，已经有八千多游客走进了西江。到我们走出观察哨，坐着电瓶车穿过人流如织、灯光明亮的主街时，李主席又说，入夜以后又进来了三千多游客，一整天超过一万了。而在放暑假以后的大热天里，游客人数几乎天天超过三万哩。

哦，烟雨西江，似乎是在告诉我们，苗寨一年四季中的每一天，都会有蜂拥而至的客人们赶来。

西江苗寨是美丽的，烟雨西江的美则是难逢难遇的。

情在贵州山水间

镇远古镇

# 镇远夜梦幻曲

　　古城镇远是有一点神秘的。神秘在哪里？初到贵州镇远的客人都会说，这么一座有着典型历史风貌的小城中，为什么会有现代化的铁路穿城而过？解答这个问题，其实就是解开镇远神秘的谜。

　　镇远最为著名的景点，青龙洞贴崖古建筑群中佛教、儒教、道教合一的庙宇中，印度的圣雄甘地年少时曾在此研究过宗教。到了60年代末、70年代初，修建湘黔铁路时，周总理特别指示，湘黔铁路途经镇远时，一定要让所有的乘客，坐在火车上就能看见高雅、奇特、优美、别致的贴崖古建筑之壮美。

记得，我第一次透过列车的车窗，见到贴崖而建的青龙洞时，心中的惊喜、震惊、赞叹真是难以言表。

道破镇远这一点神秘的谜底，其实只是解开神秘镇远的一段现代史。而有着两千多年历史的小小古城镇远，积淀下来的神秘还多着呢！比如说，镇远整座城市的形状，为什么是太极形的？被称为太极之城，穿城而过的潕阳河其S形的流向，是天然河道，还是古代人工有意为之？沿河而建的砖雕建筑群，城中遗存下来的古驿道、古关隘、古桥梁、古城垣、古民居、古巷道、古建筑园林，透视出的是怎样的历史文化信息？

又比如说，《儒林外史》的作者吴敬梓从来不曾来过镇远，为什么在他的小说里，把铁溪两岸周边的山势景色，写得栩栩如生，比到过铁溪的人描绘得更为逼真形似？正因为心中揣着一个个神秘的谜，在古城镇远的夜晚，泛舟潕阳河，才会有那种如梦似幻的感觉，才会觉得"恍然江南梦里见"的陶醉。

哦，这是夜的镇远。璀璨明亮的华灯辉映下，潕阳河清碧的流水闪烁着波光，游船无声地划向河水中央。奇了，天上的月牙儿在云层里穿行，黝黑的天幕中清晰地出现一座四官殿，噢，那是石屏山巅、峭壁危崖之上的殿宇。到了夜里，夜幕把耸峙挺立的山崖遮蔽了，唯独悬着灯彩的四官殿出现在我们的视野里，那真是出人意料的美轮美奂。身边的游人情不自禁惊喜地叫起来："这分明是天上人间，真正是人入仙境！"

游船前方，贴崖古建筑群在灯光的辉映之下，不是仙境，胜似仙境。建于古代的七孔大石桥和建于当代的跨河大桥，像两道彩虹横跨在河面上，灯光下不断地变幻着色彩。㵲阳河两岸所有徽派的砖雕楼房上，一盏盏红灯笼全都亮起来了。砖楼的阳台上、窗洞里有影影绰绰的男女，游人也在岸上兴致盎然地看着我们。

镇远城中六牌十巷中的灯笼一齐亮起来了，星河灿烂，灯河璀璨，在这一派闪闪烁烁的灯河灯海之中，最突出的是祝圣桥上的魁星阁，这幢当年为给康熙皇帝祝寿而建的楼阁，高达 15 米，三层重檐八角攒尖顶的轮廓，被串串彩灯装点得分外明丽分外妖娆。

我凝坐船头，置身于镇远之夜的一派辉煌灿烂之中，由衷地赞叹着，桨声灯影里的秦淮河，哪里能同㵲阳河相比？即使巴黎的香榭丽舍大街、纽约的时代广场、东京的银座，同有着 2000 多年历史的镇远古城来比，只怕也要感觉逊色的罢。

哦，镇远的夜，美丽璀璨的夜。

情在贵州山水间

赤水四洞沟瀑布群

# 赤水瀑布欢乐颂

写过一篇《双挂大瀑布》,写的是贵州境内两挂瀑布的景象和气势。

不料有不少读者对我道:"我们只知道贵州有黄果树瀑布,你写的另一个瀑布在哪里呀?"

甚至有在上海工作的贵州人也对我讲:"叶老师,我是贵州人,怎么没听说过你写的另一条大瀑布啊?"

其实我那篇文章里写得明明白白,除了黄果树大瀑布,贵州的另一挂大瀑布,就是赤水大瀑布。顾名思义,这挂大瀑布在赤水市（原赤水县）。

难怪很多人不知道它。一来是黄果树瀑布太出名了，除了《徐霞客游记》中有记载，黄果树瀑布就在贵州通往云南方向的公路边，南来北往的司机们都见过它，还有一个不可否认的原因，黄果树瀑布的文章被编进过语文课本，千千万万的学生都读过课本。没有见过黄果树瀑布的孩子们，也都在课本和语文老师的介绍中知道它。

赤水大瀑布就没有如此幸运了。

一来，大瀑布藏在贵州北部靠近四川省的大山深处。当年，赤水县就是紧挨着四川的一个县。红军长征四渡赤水就是想过了赤水河，到四川去。赤水大瀑布呢，又离开这条有名的河很远。而且，多少年来，这挂瀑布在当地百姓的口中，称为十丈洞瀑布。

我在贵州当知青的青春年代，听老乡说，黔北那里，靠近四川的深山里，还有一挂十丈洞大瀑布，气势壮观得很。

我顿时来了兴趣，连声问："十丈洞？这瀑布有十丈深还是十丈宽？它究竟在哪？"

讲给我听的乡村小学教师，朝着我连连摇头："离得那么远，我都没见过，只是听说壮观得很！"看见过黄果树瀑布就行了嘛，我在想，十丈洞瀑布再好看，也不会超过黄果树瀑布吧。要超过了，它现在肯定比黄果树瀑布还出名哩！

见我有些失望，他又安慰我："你想想啊，就是宽十丈，或者深十丈，一丈才是3米了，它也不能同黄果树瀑布相比嘛！"

于是我也只得打消了想亲眼目睹十丈洞瀑布的念头。

后来我在那块土地上成了作家，又在省文联工作，碰到黔北特别是赤水县到省城来的作者，闲聊之中，我就会挑起话头，问一问十丈洞瀑布。

哪晓得，很多人并不了解十丈洞瀑布。即便听说过，也坦率地告诉我，叶老师，这挂瀑布太偏僻了，离开县城，都有七八十里地呢。你从省城下去，只怕一天都到不了。话语之中，就是想打消我去看一眼十丈洞瀑布的念头。

终于让我遇见了一位赤水县的诗人，他年长我一二十岁，对赤水县的人文地理都能讲出些道道来。他告诉我，其实十丈洞瀑布早在清朝时期就有人晓得了，时任仁怀直隶厅的同知陈熙晋写过关于瀑布的一首诗。说着，他就把诗背了下来。

他说话的黔北口音重，听过一遍，我让他写下来。于是他在纸片上给我写出了这首诗：

洞深十丈锁云烟，谢监栖迟廿五年。
采木使臣归未得，山中开箐已成田。

地方上的诗人言之凿凿地告诉我,十丈洞瀑布名称的由来,就是这首诗。

陈熙晋这个清朝诗人我晓得,他写过关于茅台酒的诗,我还引用过。这首诗分明写的是他作为地方上的官员,为朝廷去选采黔北大山里的楠木,其时的所见、所闻、所感。

顺便说一句,北京毛主席纪念堂建造时的大楠木,也是从这一片山岭里选购去的。

自那以后,无论清朝、民国年间,还是新中国成立后的30多年,都没人关注过十丈洞瀑布。

直到上世纪80年代后期,国家开发赤水县凤溪河水电站,水电职工们震惊于十丈洞瀑布的壮观和气势,才在宣传建设两河口水电站的同时,也有意识地给人们介绍了十丈洞瀑布的情况。

我就是在那个时候,借着往黔北采风的机会,一次一次地去游览了十丈洞瀑布。

正如最早给我们介绍十丈洞瀑布的赤水当地人所言,这挂瀑布完全可以和黄果树瀑布媲美。它高低落差72米,幅宽80米。我站在瀑布前拍下的照片,经常被人问:"你这是在黄果树瀑布下拍的吗?"可见这挂大瀑布和黄果树瀑布确有异曲同工之妙。

记得第一次去观赏十丈洞大瀑布时,我坐的是吉普车。

那年头,北京吉普已经是县里面最好的小车了。

在弯弯拐拐的黔北山区公路上颠簸了快两个小时,才把近40公里的乡村公路跑完。下得车来,要去看大瀑布,必须步行一段朝峡谷底部的崎岖山路,前头有向导引路,后面还有人不断喊着,叶老师,你小心,路不好走,不要摔倒了。

好在我能行走弯拐难落脚的道,走得还算稳当。但也很费劲了。两只眼睛,浑身上下都关注在走路上。

累得确实够呛。陪同的朋友道,不是为了完成你的心愿,我们是绝对不会来看这条瀑布的。说得我都不好意思起来。

只在陡峭的下坡山道上拐了一个弯,只觉得一阵烟雨蒙蒙的水汽迎面拂来,把肩头、胸前、头发和脸都打湿了。这感觉我一点也不陌生,在黄果树的犀牛潭,在尼亚加拉大瀑布前,我都感受过这种朦朦胧胧的细雨般的水雾。不同的是,美国和加拿大交界处的尼亚加拉大瀑布都配有蓝色的塑料雨衣,费用就算在门票里了。在十丈洞瀑布都是不收费,不出售门票的。

几乎是烟雨迎面拂来的同时,一阵震天撼地的涛声如雷贯耳地响遍了整个山谷。抹了一把脸,睁大眼望去,只见雪浪翻滚的瀑布在水珠雾幕的陪伴下倾泻而下,其气势滔天巨浪,击石穿云。

那天摇地动的轰隆隆之声实在太大了。耳朵里什么都听不到，同行的伙伴使劲地挥着手，张大嘴喊着啥，只看见每个人都在笑。相识的和不相识的都兴奋地手舞足蹈。

一阵欢乐的颂歌从我心中油然而起，我的心在随之颤抖；我的双眼全被飞瀑的雪浪、雪沫、雪珠、雪泪耀眩，飞天而下的狂涛引得山鸣谷应，直传到九天云外，似千百虎啸龙吟。

在一阵阵欢乐颂般的瀑声中，我宛如置身于飘飘然的仙境中，这是九天落下的银河，这是蓬莱降临了尘寰，这是难得一见的壮丽景观。

赤水大瀑布，我淋了一身的水雾和细雨，我满头满脸全打得稀湿，可我始终在笑，在和一起来的所有同伴们感受着人间美景带来的欢乐。

# 春天的赤水河谷

应《酱酒天下》剧组的邀请,在 2023 年的春天里,我走进了逐渐为世人所熟知的赤水河谷。

是春天了,河谷两岸植被浓郁的岭腰间、山冈上,开满了各式艳丽的花儿。杏花的势头已过,梨花和李花的势头正旺,争相怒放着最美的色彩。而桃花,则刚刚在那儿绽开蓓蕾。还有那星星点点的,嫣红的、橘黄的、橙色的野花,在浓得让画家们都难以描摹的绿色之间,眨眼般扮演着它们年年必然到来的角色。

剧组邀请的大部分客人,都是第一次走进赤水河谷,老画家陆鹏程,在遵义地区下过乡、教过书,离开黔北至今,也有近 30 年没来了。他不时地念叨,变化太大了!著名导演张建亚,从第一天来到这里,就以惊叹的口气道:"让人惊奇了,太震撼了!说什么酒镇、酒都、酒城啊!这近百公里的赤水河谷,就是一个酱香酒世界啊!"

他说的是大实话,我们走进安酒在习水土城附近规划并

赤水丹霞地貌佛光岩

已投产的千吨酱香基地,亲眼见识了高温制曲、高温发酵、高温取酒的实践,感觉神奇至极。这一全手工操作的传统工艺,不就是酱香酒的典型代表,茅台的酿制过程嘛!

同行的电影人、小说家、编剧、出版家、书法家、美术家们,无不啧啧称奇,连声赞叹。

与他们相比,对于和贵州这一赤水河谷结缘55年的我来说,已经记不清是多少次走进其中了。我不仅在秋冬时节

九九重阳之后,一次一次来到赤水河谷,和文人们一起来采风,一起探讨为什么偏偏是这么一个河谷地带,这么一块山水土地,酿就如今名声传至海外的酱香名酒。从而在世纪之初,在茅台镇所在的仁怀市委、市政府去上海专门召开的研讨会上,明确地提出:"中国的白酒喝到了21世纪,进入了酱香酒时代。"

有人问我,你怎么会有此先见之明?现在光是小小的茅台镇,酿造酱香的成规模厂家,就有360多家。星星点点、密密麻麻,布满了全镇所有的台地。连地价都升上去了。

我说不是先见之明,只是因为我和赤水河流域有了深厚的感情。

这一次来到无忧酒业,碰到了好几位年轻时的老熟人。其中一位是40多年前,在贵州青年联合会的朋友丁德杭,杭州人啊!扎根在贵州的茅台,当年他是茅台酒厂推出的青联委员,现在他是国家级酱香酒大师,退休前还是茅台集团的党委委员。退休之后,他们和几位曾经同在茅台干过的老伙计,发誓要更上一层楼。做出茅台镇第二传奇,做一款紧随茅台的好酒！无忧酒，人生无忧，健康无忧。

品鉴会上，每个客人面前放上两小瓶酒，编上号。要会喝酒和不会喝酒的所有客人打分。结果评选公布出来，一个号得 16 分，一个号得 14 分。随后公证人宣布，两小杯酒，一杯是茅台，一杯就是新酿出来的无忧。这一结果告知了众人，这帮老伙计做出的确确实实是非常接近茅台的酱香好酒。

在《茅台酒秘史》这本书里，我写过一段茅台酒在方毅副总理直接关心之下，经过 10 年的苦战、钻研、探索、奋战之后，遗憾地承认，没有把茅台异地生产这一周总理的夙愿完成，却也无心插柳柳成荫的故事，做出了一款酒中珍品，"珍酒"的传奇。

又是 38 年过去了，珍酒现在怎么样了呢？

我们去了 1975 年建的老厂房，又去了趁着春风扩建的赵家沟新厂房。品了新珍酒，又品老珍酒。品鉴完毕，上海同去的画家、书法家、出版家、电影人纷纷说："糟了糟了，天天品这么好的酒，我们再喝平时喝的酒，喝不下去了。"

陪同着文艺家和《酱酒天下》的剧组，故地重游春天里的赤水河谷，我万万没有想到，他们不曾过分为姹紫嫣红的山花惊叹，反而会被一款又一款酱香酒所吸引，这能不能算我这一次采风的收获？

赤水十丈洞大瀑布

黄果树瀑布
荔波小七孔
西江千户苗寨
赤水丹霞
兴义万峰林
铜仁梵净山

扫码跟随
叶辛游贵州

情在贵州山水间

兴义万峰林

# 万峰林乐章

万峰林是世界自然遗产,坐落在贵州、广西、云南交界处的大山腹地。

随着贵州省的县县通高速工程于2015年底竣工,去地处黔西南兴义的游客越来越多,海内外的客人们去游览万峰林的也越来越踊跃。几乎所有的朋友,在碰到我时,都会眉飞色舞地谈到他们对万峰林的观感。

我是年轻时代看到万峰林的。那个年头,万峰林还深埋在贵州黔西南的大山深处,无论是省城贵阳,还是名城遵义的文化、旅游界人士,都没人给我提起过这一景点。

记得我第一次去兴义，清晨8点在观水路门口的省文联宿舍前出发，到达兴义的招待所时，已经是晚上9点过了。路途上整整走了13个小时。

从贵阳到兴义，那时的盘山公路里程，共计361公里。那一年，省文联刚刚进了一辆伏尔加小车，领导说，开伏尔加去吧，路途上安全点。颠簸到兴义招待所客房里住下来，我心算了一下，平均每小时，走了30公里不到。

疲倦是疲倦，不过我一点也不懊恼，反而觉得不虚此行。只因为一路驶来，我翻过了花江坡，总算爬上了72道拐。

由于高速的开通，曾经名声很大的72道拐，现在很少有人说了。

电影和电视剧《24道拐》的播出，让人只知道贵州山路的24道拐，反而把72道拐埋没了。其实在贵州，翻山越岭的大山公路中，九道拐八道拐的说法很多。我插队落户的修文县，紧挨着省城贵阳，坐长途客车，也要翻越一个叫作七道拐的大坡。记得好几个上海女知青，在车过七道拐大山坡时，晕得都吐了。

吉普车不断挂挡，好不容易盘旋着爬上72道的花江坡山巅时，我们这些坐车人都长长地吁了一口气，连声说："休息一会儿，休息一会儿。"

司机停了车,边搓着刚才紧握方向盘的双手,边对我们说:"第一次翻越花江坡,你们可以好好地看看这一面的山。"

顺着他手指的方向望去,天哪,我们看见的是一幅何等气象万千的大山的海洋图景啊!

只见高耸的花江坡前方,一览无余地坐落着千座山、万座峰。所有的苍山翠岭在阳光灿烂的照耀之下,仿佛在沸腾、在飞升,在缭绕于峰巅岭腰间的雾岚中浮动。

花江坡太高了,屹立于群山之巅的花江坡顶,山风呼啸着,拂动我们的衣服。我们互相之间,只有放大了嗓门吼,才能听到相互说些啥。

眺望着眼前千山万谷浪涌蜂浮般的壮丽景象,我只觉得整个身心听见了一阵阵雄浑苍凉的音乐在鸣奏。似乎有千万个高音喇叭将贝多芬、柴可夫斯基和肖斯塔科维奇壮丽的乐曲从风中吹来。又仿佛中国古典音乐十面埋伏中的马蹄声在腾跃。

我震惊而又愣怔地眺望着大自然神斧鬼工在眼前创造的奇景。受到深深的震撼。

司机在朝着我们喊:"可以走了吗?"

我们几个第一次过花江坡的客人几乎异口同声地对司机嚷嚷:"再看看,再看一会儿!"

其实这只是万峰林乐章的前奏。

第二天午后,当我们参加完州文联的换届会,在主人的

陪同下参观"下五屯庄园"时,隔着山野间淡淡的薄雾,如此真切地看见了万峰林梦似的乡下好景象。

雄壮宏大的乐声又在我耳畔响起,凝望着万峰林仙境般的景致,我又一次进入无语的状态,久久地欣赏着这一片和昨天在花江坡上看到时迥然不同的美景。

心中油然伴着音乐的节奏,升起按捺不住的神往之情。

我对自己说,有一天,我一定要走进万峰林的轻绡薄绫般的云雾之中,去一探万峰林中的神秘世界。

是啰,和贵州的大山结缘了半个多世纪,足足55个年头。老天没有辜负我的心愿和向往,以后的好些年间,我一次一次地自远而近、自下而上、自上而下地走进了万峰林,把万峰林的景观看了个够,看了个透彻。

原来这里是布依人世代栖居的家园。千万座山峰之间的平坝地上,盛产水稻和果蔬。挨着山路的石板坡上,顺着山

势的自然起伏，建起了一座座布依特色的农舍。一代一代布依族老乡，在万峰林这块土地上，日出而作、日落而息，过着朴实清贫的农家生活，安详自在。

脱贫攻坚的岁月中，如此大美无比的万峰林被评上了世界自然遗产，全国各地、世界各国的客人从四面八方蜂拥而来，一睹这令人心旷神怡的美景。

山水皆是画，一路都是景。春夏秋冬的花儿不同，景色变幻，不少客人觉得作为游客看一看不过瘾，干脆住了下来。

布依族乡亲说，这是客人们的热情让我们吃上了旅游饭，越过了贫困线。

而今，民宿一座比一座建得更令人流连忘返。宾馆的服务接待设施，也同大山外面的世界接轨。脱了贫的布依老乡，欢欣鼓舞地用他们勤劳聪明的脚步，行走在振兴乡村的道路上。

万峰林的乐章，奏出了更为激越和令人喜悦的音色。

情在贵州山水间

冬雪梵净山

# 云天独奏梵净山

肖邦有一首《即兴幻想曲》,今天的演奏家会以钢琴独奏来表现它,也会用笛子演奏来表现它,无论哪种形式,都会让人在短短的几分钟内得到艺术的享受。

我是50多年前在同学兼好友的家中听到这首曲子的,当即把唱片借回家中,读书之余,把唱机的声音调得低低的,一遍一遍地倾听,如痴如醉。

为什么?我也讲不透。就如同人人都会在春暖花开时想起的那首诗"春眠不觉晓,处处闻啼鸟"一样,我小时候读它,我的孙辈人现在还会读它一样。你说为什么,我也讲不透。

能讲的,只能说这是艺术的经典,经久不衰,具有永恒性。

"春眠不觉晓"是这样,"冲冠一怒为红颜"是这样,"清明时节雨纷纷"是这样,《即兴幻想曲》当然也是这样。

如若我告诉你,每一次登上贵州梵净山的山巅,我的耳畔也会随着风声响起《即兴幻想曲》的旋律,你一定会狐疑:为什么要把名曲和名山扯在一起?这几乎是风马牛不相干的事情啊。

可对我来说,这是每次攀上梵净山时都会发生的情形。

梵净山是一座名山,我听景区管委会的朋友介绍过,自从它被评上世界自然遗产名录,每年从初春到晚秋的几个月中,这里每天的8000张门票都是销售一空的。

我呢,又因和贵州结缘了半个多世纪,连头搭尾共55年,则是无数次地从前山和后山攀登过梵净山的"金顶"和"万卷书"了。

没有去过梵净山的朋友也许不知道,梵净山的峰巅之上最著名的有六大景观,其中"蘑菇石""万卷书""老金顶"和"新金顶"都是非去一看不可的美景。

年轻的时候游过梵净山,我把这座给我印象深刻的山峦写进了小说,怕有人对号入座,给它另起了一个名字:雾岚山。结果受到读者的批评:梵净山那么大,你怕啥子人对号入座啊!

我想想对的,梵净山在贵州铜仁市境内,处于江口县、印江县、松桃县三个县境的接合部,它既是贵州第一山,还是整个武陵山脉的主峰,是屹立于云贵高原朝湘西丘陵过渡的大斜坡上的巨人。我当年去湖南的凤凰玩,不就是从铜仁这边过去的嘛!

梵净这两个字,直到今天,还是周边地区不少女孩的名字哩!女娃儿生下来,起名叫吕梵净、马梵净的,都有。可见这梵净山,真是一个好名字。

春天里,我到梵净山欣赏鸽子花,那一朵朵花的花瓣比上海市花白玉兰的花瓣还要大,常常使我感觉享尽了眼福。

夏日里,我登上梵净山,出一身透汗,然后站在山巅上无论哪个位置,有舒爽的山风吹来,那种感觉真是美得让人想放声歌唱。

金秋时节,梵净山上的花儿在郁郁葱葱的绿荫中开放了,时有馥郁的花香随风弥散开来,总要引我睁大眼睛去寻找花儿在哪里。

寒冬腊月,我始终没得到机会上梵净山。可管委会的朋友告诉我,冬天的梵净山才是最美的。你在雪月里走进梵净山,真能感受"梵净"是一种怎样的境界。况且,每当我问起,地处西南的贵州省,哪里的冬天最容易下雪时,所有的

远眺凤凰山、金顶

老贵州都会告诉我,梵净山上必然会下雪。

也真是巧了,2024年元月,我真的等来了这场瑞雪。雪下得太大了,我不顾一切地抢在封山之前住进了梵净山上的招待所。那时自然客人稀少,寂寥无人,当我出入静悄悄、静悄悄的雪中梵净山,我真的觉得自己进入的是一个和人间不同的冰雪世界。那千姿百态、峥嵘奇伟的山岳冰川全都笼罩在一片白色之中,让我由衷地觉得这是一处

绝妙无比的圣地。

我在雪山、雪岭、雪峰的世界里寻觅着六大景观之一的"新金顶",纯石无土、形似巨大饭甑的"饭甑山"上遍覆白雪。陪同的当地宣传科李科长提醒我:"叶老师,你还记得吗?当地的老乡和樵夫原来都叫这山'饭甑山',因为文人墨客们来得多,又因常有人进山称这里为古佛道场,最后才定名梵净山的。"

我告诉李科长,早些年我来梵净山时,同行的文人中有一位曾在山脚下的村寨工作过,他都详细地给我介绍了。我说:"你只要把我往常季节里来时见过的那些景点一一指给我看就行了。"

大雪覆盖之下,我真的看不分明了。于是李科长立即来了劲头,他答应一声:"要得!"提高了嗓门给我边指点边介绍。

"这里是梵天一柱,金刀破峡。景点的名称就叫'金刀峡';那里是清末印江县诗人廖云鹏写诗赞过'铁索牵扶人上天'的几处景点:顶柏石、观音洞、太子石、灵官岩、天仙桥、舍身岩……我是不是讲得太快了,叶老师?"年轻的李科长说着说着停了下来,两眼盯着我问。

我说:"不快,不快,我是故地重游,这些景点自然能详。"其实我知道除了"新金顶"还有"老金顶"哩,我想他抓紧时间,把难得一见的大雪纷飞中的梵净山看个透。

真的呀,当我们从"新金顶"向北顺山脊而上时,地势高旷、视野开阔、莽莽林海、滚滚云涛的"老金顶",全都笼罩在一片雪雾、雪花之中,著名的"万卷书"仿佛被精心装帧成了雪白雪白增厚了的"银装书"典籍。以往多次上来见到的"翻天印"也变了模样。连那两个天然的圆坑"金盒"和"玉炉",亦显得更为神奇和诱人。

我还想去看看"一线天""玉皇顶",李科长指着天色道:"看不得看不得了,叶老师,你都75岁了,我还得为你的安全负责呢!要不,等在半山的尚空主任要刮我胡子了!"

"刮胡子"是贵州批评人的另一个说法。我当然只得依他的!不过我提了一个要求:"你不要说话,就让我在这雪花纷飞的老金顶上静静地伫立2分钟。"

李科长当时就闭了嘴,不解地瞪着我。我也不作解释。只为,我又一次分明听到了《即兴幻想曲》的旋律。

那是云天独奏梵净山的旋律。

梵净山自然保护区一级保护植物珙桐

黄小西吃晚饭
【集章打卡地】

扫码跟随
叶辛游贵州

黄果树瀑布
荔波小七孔
西江千户苗寨
赤水丹霞
兴义万峰林
铜仁梵净山

情在贵州山水间

# 人间最短的河

人间最短的河,在传闻中又独特又神奇,却不可到达。

当地老乡又叫它世上最短的河,从河的发源处到河的消失处,一眼看到尽头,老乡为它取名神龙河。

神龙河坐落在贵州和湖南相交的梵净山脚下。说它不易到达,是我的切身感受。梵净山是佛教名山,40多年前去贵州插队落户时,就听说了梵净山的盛名。说这山上有一种花,世上少见,盛开的时候就像白鸽子展翅欲飞;说这山上有一块石头,有人叫它千页书,有人说它是万卷书,总而言之,就像千本万本书堆在一起耸立起来,永远不会倾覆;只是,它在金顶上,十次爬上去,九次看不到它的真面目。一旦让你撞见,看到了一次,你的运气就来了。

那个时候坐火车路过湖南的新晃和贵州的玉屏,车上总有旅客说,从这里下车,再赶半天车,就能到达梵净山。可是只听见人说,从来没见人真下车去玩过梵净山。

后来我由知青变成了作家,在省城贵阳工作,走遍了全省的山山水水,唯独没有到过梵净山,只因那年头,从贵阳到梵净山所在的铜仁地区,要坐两天长途客车,中间得在山乡的小旅店里住上一晚;一来一回就得四天。到了山脚下,攀登梵净山,上山一天半,下山一天半,来回又是三天。一辈子难得到一次铜仁,总不能只爬一座山,城区要看一看,其他景观要转一转,还要和文联、作协的朋友见个面,谈一点工作,不准备上10天时间,是脱不了身的。而我那时候,在省城里还兼着一些职务,不可能丢下工作,跑出去整整10天时间。故而虽在贵州生活、工作了21年,我始终未曾到过梵净山。世上最短的神龙河,自然是听人说得神乎其神,没有亲眼目睹。

现在好了,从贵阳到铜仁,大部分修通了高速,五个多小时的车程,就能到达梵净山。

下了决心,腾出 3 天时间,不但攀上梵净山观赏了高高的峰巅上的万卷书,看见了千山净谷里白鸽般的珙桐花,终于走到了人间最短的河——神龙河畔。

不走到河跟前,难以想象,世上真会有这么短的河。当地土家族老乡告诉我,这条河头连搭尾,不过一里半长。拉着绳子细测过,就是 750—800 米。不到一公里。

世上还有比它更短的河流吗?

这地方叫云舍。在土家语里,就是"猴子喝水的地方"。我放眼望去,神龙河畔坐落着一个土家村寨,正是黄昏,夕阳把清澈的神龙河水洒出无数的金斑银点,有土家妇女,相互说笑着在河水引出的小堰塘里洗涮碧绿的蔬菜,源头那边,一个小伙子正在俯身提水,土家寨子上,炊烟袅袅,鸡犬相闻;村寨外头,田畴阡陌,郁郁葱葱的树木铺展到那边叫水银坡的山上,真是神龙河畔一派好风光。

土家族老乡说,这条人间最短的河,还有两个奇妙之处。一是河水深不可测,农闲时节,曾有 30 多个青壮小伙,每人拿出一箩筐绳索,将其连接成一条长绳,绳头绑上一块大石头,沉入潭中,想测出神龙河源头的深度。可是长绳放完了,石头都没沉到底。二是神龙河还有个怪现象,天气久晴无雨,神龙河水必涨,涨到快要溢出河沿了,天就会下雨;天气久雨不晴,神龙河水必会落潮,河水越退越少、越落越低，落到快要见到河床了，天就会朗开放晴。更难得的是，无论是涨水落潮，神龙河的流水始终淙淙潺潺，清澈见底，挑回家去饮用，甘甜可口。自古以来就是云舍土家人的生命之源。

我沿着神龙河畔的石阶信步走去，走到寨子边临近800米处，只见河水流入一条貌似沟渠的缝隙，奇了！河水流失不见了。它究竟淌到哪里去了呢？哦，人间最短的河，真是一条神奇的河。

# 该爱吗?

是问自己,也是问世人。

该爱吗?

在涉及族际婚姻的时候,这样的问题时常被提出来。

50多年前,我初到贵州接触到世居山乡的少数民族,在为创作有意识和他们交流沟通时,谈不多久,就会涉及这一话题。而且往往会被告知,无论是苗族、布依族、侗族、彝族,还是水族、土家族、仡佬族等,他们在婚姻上往往坚持同宗同族为主,异族通婚的情况是极少见甚至是不允许的。汉族的小伙子和少数民族姑娘恋爱上了,或多或少都要经历一些波折,才能走向婚姻殿堂。少数民族和少数民族之间,相恋以后提出结婚,往往会引起两个民族之间的纷纷议论,说三道四。在具体的操作程序和婚俗礼仪上,惹起大大小小的纠纷。尤其是在偏远闭塞的地方,还会引起风波,由意见不合和双方寨老固执己见闹出矛盾,乃至不欢而散,鸡飞蛋打一场空。

我还以此为题材，写过涉及民族习俗和婚姻及团结的作品。长篇小说《绿荫江畔》写的就是这一题材。

我始终以为，少数民族恋爱、婚姻伦理方面的风情，是自古传下来的，是坚守了千百年的传统，是不会变的。

像从梦中醒来一般，这些年来，每年回到贵州去，有时间深入苗寨侗村布依人家，经常饶有兴味地应邀参加少数民族的节庆活动：水族的卯节、端节，苗族的牯藏节，布依族的六月六，还有热热闹闹的婚礼——有的是嫁女，有的是娶亲。

坐在客席上喝着米酒，静静地观察着少数民族拜老人的礼节，听着她们欢乐无比的歌声，看着他们的服饰，有时候还离席加入他们尽情尽兴的舞蹈。我不知不觉地察觉，原先以为一成不变的规矩和程序，和我半个世纪之前见到的不一样了。

比如说布依族婚俗上有一个传统，新娘子正式落户到夫家那几天，她除了要随丈夫认识左邻右舍和寨子上的亲属，特别是长辈之外，还要在开初的几天一大早，就要为住在村寨上的亲属长辈家挑水，把他们家家户户的水缸挑得满满的，一来，让夫家人看看，这新媳妇是不是勤快，是不是有劳动力；二来呢，清凉的水挑进亲属长辈们的家，一边把水倒进水缸中，一边同主人家搭讪、寒暄，通过这一过程，也增进了相互的了解。30多年前的1980年代，这一传统还是司空见惯，极为普遍的。

到了今天，新媳妇们纷纷告诉我，"早不兴了，叶老师，你不晓得呀？自来水管接进了每家每户，还需要啥新媳妇上门挑水啊！"

一句话点醒了我！

是啊，顺着这一思路，仔细地在民族村寨上和他们交流、摆谈、打听，我陡然发现，原先我想当然地认为一成不变的那些风情、俚俗、礼仪、规矩、程式，也都在时代大潮的撞击之下，悄然地、不知不觉地，也像"新媳妇挑水"一样地演变了。

在贵州的世居少数民族中间，结婚成亲的当晚，有个名曰"不落夫家"的传统，那就是新娘子不和新郎同房，而是由一同来的伴娘陪着睡，睡过一晚（也有住三晚的）就回娘家，隔开几天，新郎带上礼品，再去老丈人家，拜见了岳父岳母，然后把新娘接回来圆房，至此婚礼才算大功告成。

具体的细节上有所差别，新娘回娘家住的时间也有长短，但是，"不落夫家""回门"这一传统做法，还是必须有的程序。现在这风俗还有吗？

一些年轻的姑娘、小媳妇都向我摆手："不兴了，不兴了！叶老师，结婚就成家了嘛。"也有部分村寨上的男女坦率地对我说:"现在都跑进大中城市打工,好多风俗都变了。只在回到老人身边时,我们才象征性地履行一下,为的是让老辈人高兴。"

就是传统的"相亲""说媒""订婚""订日子"等繁琐的仪式,也都简化了。

贵州的荔波县是个民族县,少数民族人口占到92%以上。很多地方,都是以布依、水、苗、瑶族为主。在荔波的民族节日中,我经常看见,水族过卯节,居住在四乡八寨的布依族、瑶族、苗族、壮族的年轻人,都会穿着各自特色鲜明的民族服装,喜气洋洋地前来参加。他们同样欢声笑语,歌舞芦笙,像过自己民族的节日一样。反之,布依族过六月六歌节,瑶族过陀螺节、盘王节,苗族过芦笙节,其他民族也都前来参加。不但爱热闹、爱玩耍的青年男女争先恐后地前来参加节庆活动,就连男女老少,都爱趁着过盛节,走乡串寨,来自己交的异族朋友家喝个酒,交交心,耍一个痛快。而未婚的小伙和姑娘们,则恣情地唱歌跳舞,趁着这一机会,寻找自己心仪的对象。

你们民族过节是这样,我们民族过节同样齐来欢庆。接触的机会多了,"对眼"的次数也就多了,就像他们"见子打子"的歌声里唱的:

> 你对我一眼，
>
> 我对你一眼，
>
> 对着对着就对上了眼……

有同宗同族相互对上的，也有异族之间对上的。那么，会不会还像几十年前我采访到的情形一样，被认为触犯族规、违背祖训、大逆不道惹出风波来呢？

不会，不会。

上点年纪的家长，无论是布依、水族还是苗族，都会以肯定的语气对我说："关键是两个娃娃自己，相互喜欢就可以。我们不多管。"

有一位布依族姑娘的妈，将近五十岁的妇女对我说："不管她嫁哪一个，只要她心里愿意，能过上靠劳动生活的日子，我当妈的都认可，至多叮嘱她几句为妇之道。"

另一个四十出头的水族姑娘的妈和自己老公相对望一眼，笑着坦然说："他们年轻人说的是来不来电，要是两边都来电，我们拦得住吗？"

"再说了，"她老公边抽烟边补充道，"水族、布依族、苗族、侗族，换上一身出门去打工的衣裳，进了城市，离开我们那么远，他们要相好，我们管得着吗？像我们这个年纪的，现在都是能不管就不管。"

"跨民族结婚，有啊！不但有水族和布依族结婚的，能干英俊，有点本事的布依、水族小伙子，还把外省的漂亮姑娘娶回山寨上来呢！"村干部在一边给我补充介绍，接着他扳着手指给我数过来，一数数了五六个省份。说着说着他笑了起来："你们那些汉族姑娘，嫁到了村寨上，才大方呢！学我们水族人酿酒，学布依族蜡染，说什么，学会了可以进城做网红饮料、网红服装。有了缘分，哪个民族都可以成为一家子！"

对我来说，这是近几年最大的收获了。我越来越清晰地意识到，四五十年前我熟悉并对具体程序了解到的民族婚俗、婚俗禁忌、族际通婚，随着时代的发展，打工潮的波及，一代一代各个年龄层次的年轻小伙和姑娘们涌进都市，正在发生着潜移默化又相当明显的变化。这一点，连偏远村寨上的少数民族老人，比我还年长的寨老们，都会点着脑壳承认：

"变了，世道变了。民情风俗也不知不觉变啰！"

该爱吗？

已经不是问题。

今天荔波民族混居地方的年轻一代，用他们正在经历的人生，证明着这一点。

# 万彩的水

万彩的水,可以说是荔波景区里最大、最吸引人的特点。而要看到这一特点,非得钻进小七孔景区不可。

这可能也是自从荔波被评上最高荣誉的世界自然遗产以来,涌进小七孔景区游览的客人们占到九成的原因。

那千姿百态的水太夺人的眼球了。

那水的色彩太迷人太有诱惑力了。

那水给人的想象力也太倍添其魔性了。以至于所有人游过荔波回来,问他对什么景色印象最深,他会说瀑布。瀑布的景色太美,太难忘。

而最难忘的,就是68级跌水瀑布。

其他地方的瀑布都是从高山上飞泻而下的,而68级跌水瀑布,是躺在河谷里向着你滚过来的。推雪拥云一般的浪花朝着人们欢笑着奔涌而来,能不让人惊讶吗?有人细数过,沿着响水河谷,自下而上地缓坡走到1.6公里的高处,遂而又不甘心地走回来,自上而下地复核,一个位置一个位置留影，一个角度又一个角度拍摄，取不尽的美景，一次次地做出笑脸。有人说，哪里有68级跌水啊，我数来数去，只有57级。一听此话，马上有人反驳，那是你数得不细致，我在心中数的，每一个跌宕都算上，七八十级都不止。还有人笑道：

"为啥说是68级呢？"

那是世代居住在这里的布依族和瑶族，喜欢6和8两个吉利的数字，以这一股长长的瀑布水，象征他们的美好愿望，祈愿他们在人世间的这种日子，永远像一年四季响水河的流水那样，长流不断。祝愿他们的生活，永远像响水河两岸繁茂常青的绿色山岭那样，郁郁葱葱，四季吉祥。

"哗哗啦啦""嘻嘻哈哈"，响水河河谷里日夜奏着这美好热切的乐曲，时而舒缓优雅，时而狂泄奔腾。那白色的水面时宽时窄，水色变幻着奇异的绿色、蓝色；瀑布飞溅起来的水珠大的如白玉兰花，小的如珠玉，晶莹透亮，欢蹦雀跃地犹如舞蹈一般。清晨和黄昏，河谷弥漫起曼妙的雾纱，白中透蓝，摄影师们会俯身占据着河岸地势，忘情地按动快门，捕捉着水雾之中如梦似幻的景致，全然不顾如潮的游客们的喧嚣、拥堵、欢声笑语，全然不顾响水河如何的伴奏。还有的游客，为这银河泻地变化万千的水色所吸引，来来回回地欣赏着形态各异、争奇斗艳的水景，在68级跌水瀑布上下，徜徉着走了好几个来回，仍不肯离去。

走累了，选择一个他自认为是绝佳的位置，坐定下来，睁大了双眼仍在贪婪地欣赏。

世上还有哪一种瀑布，能如此迷人吗？

如果说68级跌水瀑布奇妙于躺在那里供人欣赏的话，那么，小七孔景区的拉雅瀑布，让人乍一眼看到，就会不由得赞叹道：

"哦，美女瀑布！"

她那秀美优雅的模样，就如同一位披着白纱的浴后美女

在布依话里，"拉雅"恰恰就是"美丽的少女"之意。可见大多数人的感觉，和布依人为它取名时是一样的。

可我碰巧见过"秀雅少女"的另一副面貌。

2011年的初夏时节，正是荔波春汛泛滥、波涛翻涌的那几天，我进入了小七孔景区，还没走进拉雅瀑布一窥这少女的美貌，只听远处雷声隆隆，整个儿是一番排山倒海之势，我急步转过山湾，只见平时常见的拉雅瀑布，势如雪崩般横空倾泻下来，一改我记忆中的体态和飘洒之姿，而是轰然到路面上，占据了供游客行走和观赏之地的大半。

这是我难得一见的气势，一时间竟被震慑住了。我远远地站着，当下就吟出一首小诗：

> 山中涛声如惊雷，
> 林间雪瀑似花蕾。
> 布依神话说娥媚，
> 浪白更显青山翠。

这就是我当时那一瞬间的感觉。

小诗中提到的那个娥媚，正是布依神话传说中那个美丽少女的名字。

很少有人知道，在娥媚长成一个亭亭玉立的美少女那年，布依人遭遇了一场特大旱灾，田土龟裂，半坡上苞谷枯死，水田里秧苗不长，村寨上的牛羊鸡鸭干渴而死，家家户户的水缸都见了底。娥媚和寨邻乡亲们纷纷跑出去寻找水源，可是找不见啊！好些人都失望得打道回府了，不少姑娘和媳妇愁得只会掉泪。唯独娥媚姑娘，强忍着饥饿和干渴，仍在山坡上坚持不懈地寻找泉眼。她用小锤敲打着，用雀嘴锄挖着，伸出双手的十指去刨着、掏着，指甲出血了，痛得她昏厥在半坡上。苏醒过来，似有神明在暗示着她，她察觉到昏睡着的泥土十分潮湿，耳朵里又似听见了阵阵暗河淌出的水声，她再次伸出伤痕累累的十指去挖，去掘，终于，石头泥巴缝隙中出现了一个泉眼。她顾不得疲倦和肚饿，使出最后的力气，拼命地刨啊刨啊，就在她气喘吁吁地即将倒下时，她使出浑身的力气扳住一块山石,狠命地往后一扳。

轰隆一声,石头和娥媚一起被冲倒在陡峭的山坡上。

奇迹出现了,一股气浪带出一大股泉水喷涌而出,倾泻而下。水势越来越大,陷入绝望之中的布依寨得救了,方圆几十里的田土得到了瀑布水的灌溉,成千上万的老百姓获得了生机。

娥媚却为此消失得无影无踪。有人说她为救乡亲献出了宝贵的生命,有人说她升了天,当了神仙。

布依人为了纪念娥媚舍身救助乡亲,永远地怀念她,就把这漫坡的瀑布,取名为拉雅瀑布,为的是让所有人世间的朋友见到这股瀑布,就想到美丽的布依少女。

我想,今天越来越多的中外游客走进小七孔景区,看到拉雅瀑布,惊愕于她的温婉秀美时,也应该知道这个我青年时代在布依寨上听来的凄美动人的故事吧。

如果说拉雅瀑布有一股逼人的美丽的话,那么,坐落在响水河上游峰丛洼地里,四周团转的全是青山翠谷。田野里满是绿色的翠谷瀑布,则更似小家碧玉,只见高至60多米的绿荫丛中,宛如玉带贴着翠壁顺着山势淌来,山显得愈加的翠绿,水变得更白,更有不慌不忙的灵动之感。飞溅的水花旁,飘浮起薄纱般的淡雾,更会看得让人惊呆,半天才会醒过神来,留影纪念。

如若说小七孔景区里68级跌水瀑布、拉雅瀑布、翠谷瀑布各有各的形态，各有各的色彩的话，那么，走进了水上森林，挽起裤管、脱下鞋袜，就能体验到世属罕见的感受，体验到流水欢歌般的刺激。

我是被水上森林里出奇清澄碧亮的水色所吸引，毅然决然光着脚板踏进水上森林的。

正是盛夏时节，同行的上海伙伴一个个都把裤管挽得高高。带头踏进水里的老孙先是一声欢呼：

"太舒服了，下来吧，都下来呀！"

他满脸是笑地招呼着我们，露出惬意的表情。

老孙比我大三岁，他敢下，我还能不下去吗？

我的双脚踏进水上森林齐膝盖的清亮流水中时，第一感觉是刺激，透心的冰凉，在炎热的夏天里却是可以承受的冰凉，且有种从未感受过的舒服，因此瞬间就适应了。

在老孙和我的带动下，同伴们纷纷走进了水上森林。噢，那真是从未有过的快活，从未有过的体会，从未有过的放纵，只见碧亮澄明的小溪河水在我们的脚隙间流淌，一路走过去的河床石头上，长着一株一株的栎树、冬青、秋枫、重阳木，还有我叫不出名字的树木，稀奇的是它们的根系全牢牢地深植在水下的顽石上，俯身细望，这根系穿过顽石，又扎根于石头下面的河床里，形成了水中有石头，石头缝隙有树木，树木又长在水中的景观。伸手扶住一棵树干，摇撼几下，树木一动不动。这种水、石、树相偎相依的奇妙景观，我从来没有见过。

抓住了一棵树干，转过半边身子，我呼喊着没有下水的妻子照一张相，一定要把树、石头和水全照上。站定下来拍照的同时，我心中不由得冒出一个念头：

我手里紧紧扶住的这一棵树，常年在水中浸泡着，长得如此茁壮，为什么不会被冰凉的流水淹死？

岸上拿着扩音器的导游，像是看到了我的心事一般，揭开了这一问题的谜底。她说，据科学家解释，河道里溪水流动中，水中的二氧化碳排出，碳酸钙沉积下来，覆盖了河流中的地面，同时也被植物的根部紧紧包住，形成了一层保护严密的钙化层。

水上森林里树木不被淹死的秘密，原来是在这里。

这真是大自然自有其常人难得窥视的神秘一面。

让我想到《万彩的水》这个题目的，是小七孔被人拍摄最多，也最著名的一个景点——鸳鸯湖。

是鸳鸯湖的名字吉利，双双对对的情人们愿意涌来吗？

非也，鸳鸯湖岂止是年轻的情侣们愿意前来，一年四季，无论哪一个季节，走进小七孔景区，来到鸳鸯湖，湖面上总有游船，湖岸上总是人头攒动，人群拥挤，围满了各个年龄段的游客，大家站在各自选定的位置，争相摄影留念。

在鸳鸯湖泛舟，一看鸳鸯成双成对、亲密嬉戏；二看湖中的千年鸳鸯树并肩而立，相依相伴；三看湖水中的鱼儿，既有长得硕大的鲤鱼，还有难得一见的铜鱼——头小而尖，眼睛细小，嘴巴在下位。我数次来到鸳鸯湖畔，关注的都是湖水的颜色。

特别是在阳光明媚的日子，看太阳初升时湖水是一种颜色；烈日当空时，湖面又是一种闪烁金光银光之色；夕阳西斜时，湖色更变幻出迷人的色彩。看嘛，鸳鸯湖四周常绿常翠的树荫映入湖中，随着阳光从不同的角度照射着波光粼粼的湖面，湖水有时是蓝宝石般晶亮，有时是玛瑙色，有时又像紫丁香色、黑玫瑰色、翡翠色，给我的感觉是五彩夺目，怪不得鸳鸯湖又名瑶池，说的是它和天上才有的仙境可以媲美。

同样一个欣赏多彩水色的景点，就是小七孔景区这里最后的卧龙潭。

卧龙潭水夺人眼球的是直坠而下的巨幅银帘，游客们往往蜂拥在悬挂河面的巨帘前留影，上下左右，站满了摆出各种姿势欢呼着留影的人们。在拥挤的人群中，摄影之后，就觉得大功告成，往往忽视了欣赏潭水的斑斓瑰丽。

貌似平平静静的在那里的卧龙潭水，同样会随着四季光

影的变幻,给人以五颜六色交相辉映之感。一会儿潭水是深绿色的,一会儿变得湛蓝湛蓝,一会儿那水色又成了深蓝色……

这又是什么原因呢?

荔波这一典型的喀斯特地貌,山山岭岭覆盖着层层叠叠的原始森林。郁郁葱葱的大森林需要丰富的水源滋润,而大面积的森林又以它的无私涵养着水源,起到保持水土的作用。反而,水体也便显得出奇的清澈透亮。同样,山体的碳酸盐石中,碳酸钙、碳酸镁溶解到水中以后,形成大量游离的钙离子、镁离子,使水色变幻出种种我们欢欣鼓舞地看到的七彩风光。

哦,人们称呼卧龙潭是七彩潭,原来也是有原因、有依据的。

荔波的水是写不尽的。

万彩的水,是我找不到更好的形容词,写下的一种直觉。

小七孔景区里的万彩之水,只不过较为集中罢了。

其实,深入荔波的江河腹地,你还能发现更多迷人的水色。

荔波小七孔卧龙潭

# 醉歌六月六

我的长篇小说《五姐妹》中,能逮鱼、能唱歌又喜欢喝酒的布依族小伙子耿庄,凭着他那独特动听的歌声,唱得上海女知青沙海红的心颤悠悠的,不知不觉为他所吸引,后来嫁给了耿庄。沙海红作为女知青的命运,一波三折。

有相同知青经历的读者,特别是同样在少数民族村寨有过下乡经历的人,对我提出批评,说少数民族男女青年的歌声,确实好听,但也仅仅是听着的时候觉得好听罢了。像我描写的那样,唱得沙海红牵肠挂肚,唱得她心神不宁,最终还嫁给了对方,这是不可能的事。之所以有这样的故事情节,是我为了小说的需要虚构的。知青们还起哄,要我老实交代,是不是这样。

我只能说,不少知青虽然也曾在乡间接触过能歌善舞的少数民族,有的知青甚至会唱也会跳,但是他们并没有真正深入地了解少数民族的歌舞文化。具体到我描绘的桂村这么一个布依山寨,他们的了解都是肤浅的。

这就要讲到我这篇小文的标题：醉歌。

不是喝醉了酒唱歌，也不是喝醉了酒听人们歌唱，而是听着那些动人心弦的歌，陶醉其中的那种腾云驾雾的感觉。

荔波地方的布依族，也像散居黔南和全省各地的布依族一样，要过六月六，也即农历的六月初六。到了这一天，除了像过新年、过端午那样，要杀猪宰羊、要喝酒欢聚之外，和其他节日不同的，那就是以歌会友、以歌抒情。荔波六月六歌节，就是这么形成的。中老年的布依人，在歌节上畅叙亲情，边喝着酒，边唱大歌。大歌唱的是布依人的历史、民间传说和神话，若有外来客人，还会边招呼你喝米酒，边给你歌唱"六月六"的由来。此歌带有叙事的性质，故而曲调柔和舒缓、悠悠地给你道来。这类歌唱也叫"酒歌"，喝着酒，唱的唱，倾听的倾听，在这一氛围里，不知不觉地，主人和客人都会沉浸其中，身心都有一种带着三分微醺的美妙感觉。而来自四乡八寨的青年男女，唱的往往就是清朗、激越、脆亮的小歌。小歌是少男少女们最为钟情的形式，他们在歌节上充分地展现自己的才华，以歌传情，这情就是心声，面对的是心心相仪的特定对象。只有双方心中明白，歌声里带着他们对初恋和爱情的向往，带着有意的考察和盘问，表达的是他们对美好生活的向往和追求。心心相印的青年男女，就在这一过程中深情地恋上了对方，或者私订了终身。

故而到了六月六歌节，吃的是最好的酒饭，青年男女穿的更是能充分显示自己英俊和美丽的民族服饰。

年年在"六月六歌节"上评选出的公认的前三名"歌王"，会受到所有布依人的钦佩和拥戴，家家户户会把"歌王"请到自家院坝或是屋子里唱歌，让寨邻乡亲们都来学习和欣赏。鼓励更年轻的男女争当来年的"歌王"。

唱到兴头上，歌宴会通宵达旦，久久不散。

我不擅酒，之所以要写这一篇醉歌，是我听了布依姑娘唱的歌，不知不觉地就醉了，比喝了陈年茅台还觉得享受。

想想嘛，我已年过七十，听过包括世界歌王在内的许许多多男女歌唱家的演唱，尽管如此，听了布依姑娘的歌仍会有一种陶醉之感。这样的布依民间情歌，该不该用文字书写下来？

布依姑娘的情歌，和其他各民族青年男女的情歌最大的不同之处，是歌唱中很少有情啊爱啊思念啊等等字眼，也不像很多民间歌曲里带有种挑逗的谐趣意味，而是更多地采用"比兴""比喻"的方式，让听者去体会、去回味。

唱遍了全国的那一首《好花红》，是一首最著名的布依情歌，已经半个多世纪了，此歌依然受到人们的喜爱，就是一个明证。

好花红哎好花红哎
好花生在茨梨蓬哎
好花生在茨梨树哎
哪朵向阳哪朵红哎
隔河望见艳山红哎
七十二朵做一蓬哎
想摘哪朵摘哪朵哎
都是那个艳山红哎
好久不到这方来哎
朵朵鲜花遍坡开哎
金花凋了还会有哎
情意去了不再来哎
……

小七孔拉雅瀑布

    荔波的布依情歌也是这样，曲调柔和婉转，活泼而又短小。让人刚听出滋味，新的一句又来了。既无引子，又无衬句，歌词往往即兴而成，布依人说这是"见子打子"。

    在我面前唱歌的布依姑娘，穿的是一身剪裁贴身的朴素衣裳，只在前胸和衣袖处绣有几朵小花。弹奏的乐曲轻快地一响她的左手自然地往一边扬起，亮开嗓门，就用布依语脆脆地唱了起来，刚唱出一句，那清亮亮如同山间泉水般的嗓

音就引来围观者的一阵掌声和叫好声：

"好！"

她唱第二句时，就再没人鼓掌和叫好了，那声音太好听了。布依话我虽一句也听不懂，我的眼前却随着她的歌声，幻化出细雨中一对情侣，撑着花伞在竹林边散步的画面；幻化出罗密欧和朱丽叶在阳台上倾心交谈的画面；幻化出河边的月夜里男女在旁若无人的喁喁细语……

歌声是甜美、悦耳的，歌声里传递出其他地方的歌唱家所没有的那一股糯糯的撩动人心扉的情感，使得那柔柔的歌声中倍添了一股颤悠悠的滋味。

这是什么滋味呢？

我的思绪被一阵更激烈的掌声和喊好声打断了，来争睹六月六歌节的客人们纷纷叫着：

"再唱一遍，太好听了！"

"用我们听得懂的汉语唱，我们要知道你唱的是啥。"

布依姑娘微显羞涩地瞅了伴奏的小伙一眼，弹拨的乐曲一响，姑娘又用独有的普通话唱了起来："你在坡上包谷林，听没听见好嗓音？听见不用你答应，只消知晓我的心。"

布依姑娘的普通话不甚标准，可咬字清晰，大多数人都听懂了，人们又报以阵阵的叫好和掌声。我只觉得，歌词显然是即兴编的，一般了些，可经她的嗓音一唱，一个怀春少女的心事，顿时就让人们感觉到了。这是真正的天籁之音。

当人们再一次喧嚷着让她唱歌时，一大帮布依男女簇拥过来，顿时把她淹没在六月六歌节的欢乐海洋之中，锣声、鼓声、唢呐声此起彼伏，一张张男男女女的笑脸在我眼前晃动。我却仍沉浸在布依姑娘的歌声中，那甜美中带着磁性和糯音的旋律，一遍一遍在我心中回荡，似有远古的回音，似有少女之心的呼唤和真情，瞬间真有一种醉了的感觉。

随着荔波布依人生活的改善，今天的六月六歌节，又增添了原先的风俗中所没有的新内容，那就是到了这一天，女儿女婿要去岳父岳母家中，在带着外孙探望老人的同时，要为岳父母清洗棉被，要替岳父母送上一套崭新的衣裳，给岳父母带去节日的欢乐。

我心里想：荔波的布依老人们，享受到这一新的风俗时，也会像我听到布依姑娘的歌声时一样，有一种陶醉的幸福感吧。

# 加油和安龙

秋天里,陪老同学老朋友去幼儿园接他的孙子。

幼儿园里正在拔河,一声声鼓励的"加油""加油"从孩子们嘴里喊出来,显得清亮悦耳,不大的操场内一片欢腾。

接了小孙子出来,走出宽敞的弄堂时,小家伙突然向他的爷爷提出一个问题:"拔河的时候,大家为啥都要叫'加油'啊?"

我的这位相交60年的老朋友一时答不出来,转过脸来,把"皮球"踢到了我的身上,说:"爷爷答不上来。你问叶爷爷吧,他是写书的。"

小家伙顿时把脸朝着我仰起来,乌溜溜的双眼睁得大大的,问我:"叶爷爷,你知道吗?"

我只得老老实实地摊开双手,对这爷孙俩说:"加油、加油喊了一辈子,我还真不知道呢。"

没有想到,今年的元旦,应邀到贵州的黔西南州去,走进黔、滇、桂三省区接合部的安龙县,意外地获得了这个问

兴义万峰林

题的答案。

安龙县我去过多次。知道这个近50万人口的县,在贵州、在全国属于不大不小的一个县,是首批被命名的历史文化名城。一万多年前,就有人类在此活动了。万万没有想到,就是这么一个地方,却是"加油"最早让人喊出来的山地。

话得从晚清四大重臣之一的张之洞说起。1841年,张之洞的父亲张锳到此任兴义府的知府。张锳不仅是个官员,

还是一位有思想、有追求、有抱负的知识分子。来到这道路遥远的黔、桂、滇三省交界之地，他一如既往地像在他处当官时一样，重教兴学。他认为要振兴中华、重振伟业，让中国摆脱积贫积弱，首先得有人才。而要出人才，就得兴教育。他在兴义府（治所在安龙）创建了兴义府试院，重建了珠泉书院，"劝捐"倡修册亨书院、普安的盘水书院。册亨、普安都是兴义府下属的县。

为鼓励贫困家庭的孩子潜心读书、刻苦钻研、认真思考，他令府衙里的小吏，挑着一担灯油，晚上在兴义府城（今安龙县城）的大街小巷里掌灯巡游。看到哪户街坊家里还亮着灯，就敲门进屋，只要见到屋里有人在挑灯夜读，挑着油担子的衙吏便会进屋去，给主人家的灯油瓶子里加满灯油，以此鼓励读书人挑灯夜读，不要担忧灯油会燃尽。

知府鼓励读书人添加灯油的故事，一传十、十传百地就传开了。一时在百姓中传为佳话，也成为家长们鼓励自己孩子读书的动力。用功读书之风蔚然传遍城乡，一时间，在安龙，在兴义府各县，出现一股旷古未有的兴旺学习景象。尤其是贫困的农家子弟，更是挑灯夜读成风。那些家庭富裕的人家，就更不用说了。"书中自有黄金屋"，读书本就是他们以后博取功名利禄之道啊！

我在安龙著名的荷塘边散步时，在夕阳西斜的招堤上，还遇到了两个身着清朝衙吏服装的巡堤人，他俩一人挑担，一人手中也拿着一把油勺。我不由笑问："这是为什么？还要给小学生家里添灯油吗？"

说着，顺手打开了桶盖。桶里装的不是油，而是一些芝麻糖、花生糕、饼干、桃酥等零食。我笑道："不加灯油，加的是点心啊！"

一位衙吏打扮的男子笑着告诉我，张锳、张之洞父子鼓励兴义府人添灯油的故事，在我们这里家喻户晓。这会儿不正是周围的中小学放学的时间嘛，我们每天在这时候到招堤上来，一是提醒贪玩的孩子们早点儿回家做作业，给他们送点心；二来呢，招堤国家湿地公园，本就是4A级景区，这当儿，又是游客们来得最多的时候，看到我们这身晚清时期的打扮，外来的游客们都会像你一样，来问我们是怎么回事儿，我们也正好宣传了"加油文化"。

好一个"加油文化！"

原来如此，一旁马上有当地人插话："为自己加油，为他人加油，为正从事的事业加油，也是当今需要的啊！"

我当时就想到了上海老同学老朋友那个小孙子，加油、加油的出处，原来是在这儿哩！

不过，兴义府安龙县的"加油文化"，其意义不仅仅是回答了"加油"两个字的出处，更是有着深远的意义。

那是我走过招堤、步上半山亭时，看到亭柱上的一副对联时，联想到的。对联写道：携酒一壶，到此间畅谈风月；极目千里，问几辈能挽河山。

我在对联旁坐下来，浮想联翩：鸦片战争之后，正是所谓的"五口通商"时期，中国人在洋枪洋炮威逼之下，签署了一系列不平等的条约，民不聊生……在如此大形势下，张锳、张之洞父子先后兴办各种书院，留下广为流传的"加油文化"，其意义是远比这件事令人深思的。

加油、加油！我们不仅仅是在各类比赛中习惯性地喊喊而已，更是要脚踏实地地加油干呐！

情在贵州山水间

兴义万峰林

# 我写贵州山水

　　1969年的4月2日,天已经黑下来,我和800名上海男女知识青年,坐着火车开进了小小的贵定车站。广播里通知我们中的462名将要去修文县的知青下车,吃过一顿以饼充饥的晚饭,我们住进了贵定中学的教室。

　　在排队一路摸黑走进贵定中学时,我只觉得这个县城的四周都是山。晚上躺在课桌椅拼起来的铺位上,我感觉自己迷迷糊糊地睡在大山的怀抱里。4月3日晚上,我们在久长人民公社十字街头的一座茅草盖顶的旅社二楼对付了一晚。4月4日又坐了一段路的卡车后,沿着山间小路走进了我插队落户的寨子。

行程匆匆，心急慌忙，一路颠簸，也没工夫和心情去细细观察山乡里的一切。直到在这个叫砂锅寨的村落里住下来，随着老乡们参加集体劳动，才认真地慢慢熟悉山寨的农务、道路、沟渠，还有无穷无尽的、一眼望不到边的座座山峰。说来好笑，好几次我试图站在高一点的地方去数数一共有多少座山，但是试了几次，我无奈地意识到，要想数清楚我生活的地方到底有多少座山，是徒劳的，因为光从一个方向望出去，一直望向目力不逮的山峦边上，阳光照耀之下，还是能看见一座座山的影子。这个时候，我才真正体会到，苍山如海这个词的真正含义。

那些年里，人们只要一提及贵州，任何人都会脱口而出："天无三日晴。"

知识分子这么说，工人这么说，官员也这么讲。弄堂里有文化或没有多少文化的人都这么说。其实，十个人这么说，九个人没有去过贵州，只不过这五个字太好记了，讲起来像顺口溜：天无三日晴，地无三尺平。

后来在贵州山乡里久住下来，才真正领略和体会到了贵州的大山和水的关系。除了老天喜欢下雨、下大雨、落暴雨，随风飘散着细毛雨，还有老乡们所说的那种"长脚雨"，它似乎落得不大也不小，不疾也不慢，这是随着山谷里的风，飘过来飘过去，凉悠悠、湿乎乎的。你以为它要停了，它却仍然在往下落;你以为它下大了,它落到人的脸上,却似乎没甚感觉。

那年头我仍然写日记,特殊年代的关系,我只写气象日记。整天地在脑子里琢磨,怎么来形容天天落的雨。

雨落在山上,在沟沟里汇成水流;水流顺着山坡淌下来,渐渐形成乡里的溪流。溪流里的水在晴天里几乎是无声的,而且清澈澄明,能映出蓝天白云,映照出周边的一座座山。只在雨下得大时,溪流水才会发出响声,那种咕咕噜噜的、哗哗啦啦的响声。

半山坡上响起洒落声,那必然是山泉。从高高的山上直落而下,那又是飞瀑。煞是好看。呼隆隆的似从远方滚动而下,遇到悬崖陡壁直泻而下的,那就是瀑布了。贵州最有名的瀑布是黄果树大瀑布和赤水大瀑布,原来叫作十丈洞。

瀑布、清泉、溪流、大河,还有江水,都和贵州山地有关系,和贵州山地的气候有关系,和贵州特殊的喀斯特地形有关系,和山里的溶洞、暗河有关系。这种暗河,也是贵州山地的奇妙景象。在偏远山乡,沿着溪流走,走着走着,不知不觉间,刚才还在身旁陪伴你的溪流,忽然不见了。张眼四顾,都不知溪流淌到哪儿去了?每当这时候,当地人就会告诉你,水淌到暗河里去了,没关系的,水在暗河里淌着淌着,不知会在哪个洞口,腾跃而出,流到江里去了。

143

问是什么江?

南北盘江啊,乌江啊,都柳江啊!别以为这些贵州山地的江和你没关系,细细地追究一下,都柳江、南北盘江的水,最终都流进我们国家的第三大水系——珠江流域去。而乌江水呢,直接就流进长江的上游。

真正和贵州山地的水没关系的,是黄河流域。可是这话仍不能和贵州山地的苗族、布依族老乡们讲,他们会言之凿凿地告诉你,他们的祖先原先就定居在黄河流域,是那里的原住民。只不过,沧海桑田,世事大变,我们迁徙到山里来了……

这是另一篇小文的题目了。总结一句,结合贵州山水间居住的各族老乡,其实是能找出很多话题来说的。

# 金彩妥乐村

## 一

在和我结缘了55个年头的贵州省,有一座年轻的城市,那就是六盘水市。

我说六盘水市年轻,是我记得很清楚,1978年六盘水地区改为六盘水市。那一年我还是知青身份,还没有离开农村。

早在20世纪70年代,我们这帮知青就很关注六盘水地区的消息。只听说这里盛产优质的煤矿,很多煤炭挖出来露天堆着,来不及运出来,时有煤炭自燃的情况。那多浪费啊!

后来又听说挨着盘县的六枝、水城有铁矿石,政府于是决定利用当地煤炭和铁矿建立钢铁厂,就地消化煤炭和铁矿石。为此,特地以六枝、盘县、水城为主体,建立六盘水地区。20世纪70年代末,六盘水地区改称六盘水市。

六盘水市不像其他地方,集中在一个地域,而是相互之间离得有点远,水城以钢铁厂为主,六枝是主城区,盘县以产煤炭为主。不过,历经差不多半个世纪的开采,我当年下过的火铺矿煤炭开采得差不多了,已经歇了下来。当地正在向纵深掘进,开发更多更优质的煤炭。

盘县乘着改革开放的东风,进一步搞全面的开放,而不是像原来那样一业独大。机遇也跟着来了,2013 年,盘县改成盘州市。2015 年,贵州实现了县县通高速公路。如今,上海至昆明的高铁,在盘州也设了一站,大大便利了当地人的出行。随着越来越多的人走进这里,大家很快发现,此处不单单有丰富的煤炭资源,而且还有独一无二的"宝"啊!

这个"宝",就是盘州石桥镇妥乐村的古银杏树。光是妥乐这个小村寨,就有古银杏树一千多棵。

初次听到这个数字,吓了我一跳。

60 年前,我在上海的徐汇中学读书。离校门不远,栽着一棵银杏树。一个调皮的同学爬上树去折下一根嫩枝,不仅受到班主任痛斥,还在全校的广播里受到批评。训得这位同学在几个月内抬不起头来,引得全校议论纷纷。

不少同学不解,只是折了一根树枝,至于吗?老师郑重其事地对我们说,银杏树是国宝!全上海也没有多少,怎么可以随便毁坏?

这件事，给我们的印象十分深刻。

在妥乐，竟然有这么多古银杏，怎么不让我惊叹！

多年里，我一次次走进妥乐，一次次感悟妥乐，拍摄纪录片《岁月未蹉跎》，还在妥乐取了很多景。

## 二

哦，妥乐，真是一道美不胜收的风景。

第一次走进妥乐，我就觉得妥乐的风景美得出奇。

奇在哪儿呢？一位游客拿着他的相机要我看，说："你看，随便在妥乐拍几张照片，竟然每一张都像油画。"

我定睛望去，游客不是自夸，在他的取景框里，一张张照片，都像被精心涂抹了诱人的金黄色。

只匆匆看了几眼，我就觉得这些照片就像我在俄罗斯的美术馆里看到的"金色系列"的油画。眼前这位游客，虽然不是专业的摄影家，他拍下的照片竟然如此之美。我不得不承认，妥乐的风光有她的独特性，特别是在金秋时节。

于是，我走进了妥乐的风景里。到过妥乐的人都对我说，妥乐最美的景致是小桥、流水、人家。

还有人对我说，你得占据一个好位置，把小桥、流水、人家看个够。

我却觉得，走进小桥、流水、人家，任何一个位置，任何一个角度，都能拍下一张出人意料的风景照。这可不是背景上的一丛鲜花、一座山峰、一株老树，或是某个建筑那样的风景照。在妥乐小桥、流水、人家的景致里，你能看见潺潺的溪水淌来，你能看到小桥优雅地占据着画面，你还能看到妥乐老乡摆着的白果摊，摊主坐在稻草编的圆凳上，正在向游客介绍着什么，而游客的巴掌里，正放着几颗白果。

这哪里是一般的风景照片啊！这是一幅妥乐人的生活画卷，是一幅可以拿到大城市的画廊里展出的摄影作品，说不定还能得奖哩！

一位妥乐的老农告诉我："不要小看这么一张照片啊，这就是我们妥乐人生活的地方。我们天天待在银杏林里，我们吃着银杏林的果实，享受着银杏林的风景。当然，我们同样珍惜着银杏林，保护着银杏林。每一个小娃娃生下来，我们就对他说，这银杏林就是我们赖以生存的家园。"

真的，这是美好的家园，是美好的理念，更是美不胜收的风景。

## 三

我把这点感受对一位美术家说的时候，他当即提高声气

道:"妥乐岂止是美丽的风景,那地方就是一幅画。我一直想为妥乐创作一部作品,可去了多次,画了几幅,我都不满意,不敢示人。"

"为什么?"我不由得问,甚至还想去他的画室里看看。

美术家沮丧地摇头摆手:"画出来一看,嗨,还不如我作为素材拍下来的照片好,我哪敢拿出来给人看啊!"

我激了他一句:"那你就打退堂鼓了?"

他一怔,继而一脸严肃地对我道:"妥乐这么奇妙的风景素材,是要由当代世界级的大画家来完成的。像我这种水平的,画不出来。"

我瞅着他,这家伙,平时可是自视甚高的呀!但看他认真的眼神,我觉得他对我说的,是肺腑之言。

是啊,别看妥乐只是个小小的村落,可像小桥、流水、人家这样的打卡点就有好几处,无数的游客和专业人士慕名而来,从各自的角度,从常人想象不到的方位,拍摄下数不清的美景。

可以说,每一幅摄影照片就是一幅画,况且这些画上的景观,带着人与自然的沟通。端详着妥乐特有的农舍,每一幢都相距不远,每一幢都是青砖绿瓦,最难得的是,农舍都和房前屋后的古银杏相映成趣。难怪美术家会感觉在创作上无从下笔,即使画了多幅,也不愿示人了。

不过，美术家的大实话，也引起了我的思索。俄罗斯大画家列宾对高尔基说过，和《伏尔加河上的纤夫》一样，为了创作"金色系列"的画作，他走遍了俄罗斯大地，风餐露宿，观察、感受、思索、捕捉灵感。

法国大画家莫奈为画出超过他的名作《日出》的作品，举家从繁华的巴黎搬到艾普特河边的小镇上，天天坐在艾普特河畔，观察水面上的睡莲，终于绘制出了举世闻名的《睡莲》系列油画。

我想起了一位旅居美国的画家朋友，前几年他回国时在西藏住了两个月，画了一套以雪山为背景、名为"银色系列"的组画，获得了不错的反响。

为朋友高兴的同时，我提醒他，你下次回来，我陪你到妥乐去，你一定得创作一组"金色系列"，让我们贵州的妥乐村，永远地留在你的作品中。

他一口答应，可随后发生了疫情，一切就拖延下来了。为了提醒他，我发去了一张与沈嘉蔚的合影。沈嘉蔚当年在黑龙江当知青时，画过一幅《为我们伟大祖国站岗》的画，印行了数百万张。如今，沈嘉蔚已是世界驰名的画家。我想告诉这位画家朋友，你不履行诺言，为妥乐画一组"金色系列"，我就要另请高明了！

之所以这么做，是因为我觉得该为如此美丽的妥乐做一点事儿，让妥乐的名声传播得更远，更为世人所知。

## 四

妥乐，妥乐，写了半天妥乐，妥乐两字，究竟是什么意思呢？

我和妥乐村寨里的老乡相坐品茗时，曾请教过妥乐是什么含义。老乡笑着说，这是我们这里少数民族的发音，意思嘛，就是美得像宝石，像水晶一样的地方。于是我说，能不能概括成风景如玉的地方？他们连连点头，有的说"要得"，有的说"就是这个意思"。

其实，我把妥乐形容成风景如玉，也是不甚准确的，人们珍爱的玉石往往小巧玲珑，而妥乐的面积却很大。最早去的时候，当地人给我介绍，说妥乐一共有1150棵古银杏树，后来又说，300年以上树龄的古银杏，细细清点以后足有1400多棵了。

后来我再去妥乐，当地人说银杏远远不止这个数了。妥乐及周边的老乡，看到一年年有这么多中外人士到这里来争相观赏、亲近银杏树，于是他们又新栽了很多银杏树，周边的许多村寨，也纷纷栽起了被誉为"公孙树""夫妻树""母子树"的银杏树。粗略统计，方圆村寨的山山岭岭上都栽满了银杏树，约有数万株。

在这被银杏树包围的村寨里，还流传着很多趣闻。

其一，站在高处，透过金黄的银杏树梢，隐约可见两坡顶的近百幢农舍里，没有一户的床上挂有蚊帐，故而有"好个妥乐村，蚊虫永不生"的谚语。竟然还有人编轶事说，这是乾隆皇帝微服私访时御封的话。

其二，不止一个老乡对我说，1000株以上的古银杏树林里，绝大多数是母银杏树。一棵棵都生长得秀美飘逸，多么诱人。她们这是为了吸引公银杏树的关注啊！因为一大片银杏林中，只有两棵是公银杏树……

"两棵？"第一次来的时候，我伸出两个手指惊问。

老乡忍不住笑了："典型的'一夫多妻制'，是不是？不过足够了，两棵公银杏洒落的花粉，风儿一吹，保证每一株母银杏都能受益，结出丰硕的白果。"

近两年，我又走进妥乐。问老乡，银杏树的数量增加到了数万，还是只有两棵是公的吗？

老乡连声说："增加了，增加了一倍多了，现在共有五株是公银杏了。"

"哈哈！"我也随之笑了，"这五株公银杏的功劳可真不小。"

"古银杏林的功劳真不小哩！"老乡正色道，"叶老师，我们家园里的这些古银杏景观，入股了村合作社，村合作社和旅游公司合作，年年给入股的农户分红呢！"

老乡这话一下子提醒了我，盘州市的相关领导给我介绍，由于妥乐的古银杏景区美得引人入胜，吸引得"中国－东盟国际产能合作暨中国对外投资洽谈妥乐分会"也在这里举行。来自泰国、柬埔寨、马来西亚、缅甸、菲律宾、老挝等国家的客人和企业家们聚首在古银杏树下，共襄盛会，共赏美景，共寻金色合作。

## 五

坐西朝东，依山傍水的农舍，掩映在古银杏树的光影、光斑里，组成了妥乐特有的"村中见树，树中见村"的美妙景象。这景象令人惊叹，这景象更令人陶醉。很多本想到这里来走马观花的客人，都舍不得离开，有的甚至还想多住几天，充分享受晨曦和晚霞，享受每个景点带来的喜悦。

喜欢民族服饰的姑娘小伙，可以换上符合自己心愿的民族服饰，并在游览过程中了解少数民族的风情民俗。这里安装了自动摄像机，为游客们提供即时视频拍摄服务，让他们和亲人、友人分享欢乐。在农家乐里住下来，享用农家的美食，品咂一口又甜又酸又带点回味的美酒，男女老少的客人都会乐得笑个不停。在推动传统煤炭产业向绿色生态旅游转型的过程中，妥乐村不仅走在盘州市的前列，还走到了贵州全省的前列。

所有在春季、夏季来妥乐的人们，在离去的时候，都会收到这里的男女老少发出的盛情邀约：要感受妥乐仙境般的美，要看现实中的童话世界，请你们在深秋时节再来，带着你们的亲人朋友，那种情韵和味道，会让你们怀念很久很久。因为那就是一个金彩妥乐村！

有诗人对我说，叶老师，妥乐不仅是一个景区、一幅画，妥乐也是一首诗啊！是意味隽永的诗、是百读不厌的诗、是回味悠长的诗。

有散文家对我说，叶老师，你别听诗人的，几行诗怎能写尽妥乐的美。妥乐是一篇流传千古的散文，受历史和时间所限，唐宋八大家都没到过妥乐。为妥乐写下能流芳百世的诗篇和散文，这责任理所应当地落在我们这辈文人的身上。

同行的一位作曲家说，你们都从自己的艺术样式出发。说妥乐是一首诗，要写出诗来；说妥乐是一篇美文的，要用生花妙笔，带头写一篇啊！

诗人和散文家反驳道：听这话，你不同意我们的看法呀！那你说说，妥乐是什么？

众人的目光不约而同转向作曲家，作曲家当即红了脸，连连朝众人摆手："我也从自己的职业出发，我觉得妥乐就是一首歌……"

诗人截住他的话："那你写啊！"

散文家随即附和："写一首歌也很好，尽快传唱出去。"

作曲家脸红得更甚了："可是、可是……这首歌不容易写好。"

始终不声不响的画家，是上海静安书画社的副社长，见我瞅了他一眼，他淡淡一笑道："我赞成你一开头说的话，妥乐是一幅画，但这是一幅有着五光十色彩影的画，是灵动的画，是有山有水有人物的立体的画。"

众人被他的话吸引住了，纷纷围住了他，有人还小声嘀咕："你是画家，你动笔呀！"

画家做了个否定的手势："我辈不行，叶老师的思路是对的，得请国家级的，甚至有国际声誉的大画家来创作。"

诗人纳闷地说："到哪里去找啊……"

"故而，我建议——"副社长认真道，"叶老师写一篇妥乐的文章，登在报纸上，告诉你们，好画家都是爱看美景的，说不定就有人接二连三来了。"

这下好了，所有人的目光都转到我脸上来了，不表态是不行了，我只得说："我试试吧。"

我这么答应，就是想吸引更多更出色的艺术大家走进妥乐，爱上妥乐。

with colorful colors and shadows, a smart painting, a three-dimensional painting with mountains and rivers and people."

The crowd was attracted by his words, one after another surrounded him, some people also whispered, "You are a painter, start writing!"

The painter made a negative gesture, "We can't, Mr. Ye's thinking is right, we have to invite national and even international reputation of the great painter to create."

The poet wondered, "Where can I find it?"

"Therefore, I suggest," the vice president seriously said, "Mr. Ye write a Tuole article, published in the newspaper. Good painters are fond of watching beautiful scenery, maybe someone will come."

Well, everyones eyes turned to my face, so I had to say, "I'll try."

I promise this, hoping to attract more and better artists to enter Tuole, fall in love with Tuole.

you miss for a long time. Because that is a golden Tuole Village!

A poet said to me, "Tuole is not only a scenic spot, a painting, Tuole is also a poem! It is a meaningful poem, a poem that is never tired of reading, and a poem with a long aftertaste."

Some essayist said to me, "Don't listen to the poet, how can a few lines of poetry write the beauty of Tuole. Tuole is an essay for ages, and since the Tang and Song masters never visited Tuole, it's up to us to pen an immortal poem or essay to honor its beauty."

A fellow composer said, "You all started from your own style of art. If you say Tuole is a poem, then write a poem; If you say Tuole is a beautiful article, then use brilliant pen, take the lead to write an article!"

The poet and essayist retorted, "Listen, you don't agree with us! So tell me, what is Tuole?"

Everyone's eyes turned to the composer, the composer immediately blushed, repeatedly waved to everyone, "I am also from my own career, I think Tuole is a song..."

The poet stopped him, "Then you write!"

The essayist then echoed: "It is also good to write a song, and sing it as soon as possible."

The composer blushed even more, "But, but... It's not an easy song to write."

The painter, who has always been silent, is the vice president of Shanghai Jingan Calligraphy and Painting Society. Seeing me look at him, he smiled faintly and said, "I agree with what you said at the beginning, Tuole is a painting, but it is a painting

5

Facing the east, the farmhouses near the mountain and the water, were hidden in the shadow of the ancient ginkgo tree and the light spot. All of there composed of Tuole's unique "see the tree in the village, see the village in the tree" wonderful scene. The sight is breathtaking, and the sight is even more intoxicating. Many of the guests who wanted to come here for a quick look are reluctant to leave, and some even want to stay for a few more days to fully enjoy the morning and sunset, and enjoy the joy brought by each scenic spot.

Girls and boys who like ethnic costumes can change into ethnic costumes that meet their wishes, and learn about the customs of ethnic minorities during the tour. Automatic cameras are installed here to provide visitors with instant video shooting services, so that they can share the joy with their relatives and friends. Tourists can stay in the farmhouse, enjoy the food of the farmhouse, taste the sweet and sour wine with a bit of aftertaste, men, women and children will be happy and laugh. In the process of promoting the transformation of the traditional coal industry to green eco-tourism, Tuole Village is not only in the forefront of Panzhou City, but also in the forefront of Guizhou Province.

All the people who come to Tuole in spring and summer will receive a warm invitation from men, women and children here when they leave: to feel the fairyland beauty of Tuole, to see the fairy tale world in reality, please come back in late autumn with your relatives and friends, the charm and taste will make

情在贵州山水间

asked in surprise.

The fellow couldn't help laughing, "Typical 'polygamy', isn't it? But it's enough. The pollen from the two male ginkgo trees, when the wind blows, ensures that each female ginkgo tree can benefit and produce a rich ginkgo fruit."

Two years later, I went back to Tuole. I asked fellow villagers, the number of ginkgo trees has increased to tens of thousands, or only two are male?

Fellow villagers said, "Increased, increased more than doubled, now a total of five are male ginkgo."

"Ha ha!" I also laughed, "These five male ginkgo can really do their job."

"The ancient ginkgo forest does a lot for us!" Fellow villagers said, "Mr. Ye, these ancient ginkgo landscapes in our home, have invested in the village cooperative, the village cooperative and the tourism company cooperate pay dividends to the villagers who have invested in it every year!"

My fellow villager suddenly reminded me that the relevant leaders of Panzhou introduced to me that due to the attractive beauty of Tuole's ancient Ginkgo scenic spot, the "China—ASEAN International Production Capacity Cooperation and China overseas Investment Fair Tuole Session" was also held here. Guests and entrepreneurs from Thailand, Cambodia, Malaysia, Myanmar, the Philippines, Laos and other countries gathered under the ancient ginkgo trees to enjoy the grand event, enjoy the beauty and seek golden cooperation.

126

Tuole, the local people introduced me, saying that they found over 1,400 ginkgo trees that were more than 300 years old.

Then I went to Tuole, and the locals said there was more than that. Tuole and the surrounding villagers, seeing so many Chinese and foreign people come here year after year to admire and get close to the ginkgo tree, so they have planted a lot of new ginkgo trees, many surrounding villages, have also planted known as "Gongsun tree", "husband and wife tree" and "mother and child tree" ginkgo trees. According to rough statistics, there are tens of thousands of ginkgo trees planted all over the mountains and ridges of the villages.

In this village surrounded by ginkgo trees, there are many interesting stories.

First, standing at a height, through the golden gingko treetops, you can faintly see the hundreds of farmhouses on the top of the two slopes, not a single household has a mosquito net on the bed, so there is a proverb "In the good Tuole village, mosquitoes never give birth". Even some people made up anecdotes that this was the Qianlong Emperor's words during a disguised visit.

Second, more than one fellow told me that in the forest of more than 1,000 ancient ginkgo trees, the vast majority are female ginkgo trees. The trees all grow beautiful, elegant, and attractive. They are trying to attract the attention of the male ginkgo tree! Because in a large ginkgo grove, there are only two male ginkgo trees...

"Two?" The first time I came, I held up two fingers and

情在贵州山水间

Guizhou will remain in your works forever.

He said yes, but then the epidemic happened, and everything was delayed. To remind him, I sent a photo of myself with Shen Jiawei. When Shen Jiawei was an educated youth in Heilongjiang Province, he painted a picture of *Standing Guard for our Great Motherland*, which was printed in millions of copies. Today, Shen Jiawei is a world-renowned painter. I want to tell my painter friend that if you don't keep your promise to paint a "gold series" for Tuole, I'll have to find someone else!

I did this because I thought I should do something for such a beautiful Tuole, so that Tuole's fame can spread further and be known to the world.

4

After writing so much about this place, what does the name really mean?

Over a cup of tea with someone from the village of Tuole, I asked what Tuole meant. The fellow said with a smile, "this is our minority pronunciation here, meaning, is beautiful like a gem, like a crystal place." So I said, "Can it be summarized as a place with beautiful scenery?" They nodded repeatedly, some said, "That's it," and someone said, "That's what it means."

In fact, my description of Tuole as a landscape like jade is not very accurate, people's precious jade is often small and exquisite, and the area of Tuole is large. When I first went to

It can be said that every photo is a painting, and the landscape on these paintings brings the communication between people and nature. Looking at the unique farmhouses in Tuole, each one is not far from each other, each one is green brick and green tile, and the most rare is the harmony between the farmhouses in front of the trees and the ancient ginkgo tree. No wonder artists feel unable to write in the creation, even if they have painted many pictures, they are reluctant to show people.

However, the artist's great truth also caused me to think. The great Russian painter Ilya Repin told Gorky that, like the *Barge Haulers on the Volga*, in order to create the paintings of "Golden series", he traveled the land of Russia, eating and sleeping in the open, observed, felt, thought, and captured inspiration.

French painter Claude Monet in order to paint more than his famous work "Sunrise" series, moved the family from the prosperous Paris to the Apte river town, sitting on the Apte river every day, observing the water lilies on the water, and finally drew the world famous "Water Lilies" series of oil paintings.

I am reminded of a painter friend who lives in the United States. A few years ago, when he returned to China, he lived in Tibet for two months and painted a series of paintings called "Silver Series" with snow-capped mountains as the background, which was well received.

While happy for my friend, I reminded him that the next time he come back, I will accompany he to Tuole, and he must create a group of "golden series", so that our Tuole Village in

3

When I said this to an artist, he immediately raised his voice and said, "Tuole is not only a beautiful landscape, it is a painting.I had always wanted to create a work for Tuole, but I went many times and painted several paintings, I was not satisfied and dared not show them."

"Why?" I asked involuntarily, and even wanted to visit his studio to see there paintings.

The artist shook his head and waved his hands in frustration, "When I draw it out and see, hey, it is not as good as the photos I took as the references, I dare not take it out to show people!"

I dared him to say, "So you're backing down?"

He was startled, and then said to me with a serious face, "Tuole is such a wonderful landscape reference which is to be completed by a contemporary world-class painter. At my level, I can't draw it."

I looked at him, this guy, usually think highly of himself! But with the earnestness in his eyes, I felt like he was speaking to me from the bottom of his heart.

Yes, although Tuole is only a small village, there are several scenic spots such as Bridges, water and people, countless tourists and professionals come here, take countless beautiful photos from their own angles and perspectives most people wouldn't think of.

autumn.

So, I stepped into the landscape of Tuole. People who have been to Tuole have told me that the most beautiful sceneries of it are the small bridge, the water, and the people.

Someone said to me, you have to find a good position, to fully see the small bridge, water, people.

I feel that walking into the bridge, the water, the family, any position, any angle, can take an unexpected scenery photo. This is not a picture of a bush of flowers, a mountain peak, an old tree, or a building in the background. In the view of Tuole Bridge, water and people, you can see the stream flowing, you can see the bridge gracefully occupying the picture, you can also see the ginkgo stalls of Tuole people, the stall owners sitting on a straw stool, is introducing something to tourists, and the tourists' palm, is placing a few ginkgo.

This is not a general landscape photo! This is a picture of the life of the Tuole people, a photograph that could be exhibited in a gallery in a big city, maybe even win a prize!

An old farmer in Tuole told me, "Don't look down on such a picture, this is where we live in Tuole. We stay in the ginkgo forest every day, we eat the fruits of the ginkgo forest, enjoy the scenery of the ginkgo forest. Of course, we also cherish and protect the ginkgo forest. When a little baby is born, we tell him that this ginkgo forest is our home that sustains us."

Really, this is a beautiful home, a beautiful philosophy, and a beautiful landscape.

情在贵州山水间

Many students did not understand, just broke a branch, as for? The teacher solemnly told us that the ginkgo trees are national treasures! There weren't many in Shanghai, how could we destroyed them?

We were deeply impressed by this event.

In Tuole, there are so many ancient ginkgo trees, why don't you surprise me!

Over the years, I walked into Tuole again and again, shooting the documentary "Time has not wasted", and also took a lot of scenes in Tuole.

2

Oh, Tuole, what a beautiful sight.

The first time I walked into Tuole, I thought the scenery was surprisingly stuming.

A tourist showed me his camera and said, "Look, I just took a few pictures in Tuole, and every picture looks like a painting."

The tourist was not boasting, in his viewfinder frame, one photo after another, like being carefully daubed with attractive gold.

After only a few cursory glances, I felt that these photographs resembled the "Golden Series" paintings I had seen in Russian art galleries. This tourist, although not a professional photographer, took such beautiful photos. I have to admit that Tuole's scenery has its own uniqueness, especially in the golden

120

Liupanshui City is not like other places, concentrated in a region, but a little far away from each other, Shuicheng is based on steel plants, Liuzhi is the main urban area, Pan County is mainly known for producing coal. However, after almost half a century of mining, the coal mine that I used to mine has been exhausted, and has stopped. The region is digging deeper to develop more and better coal reserves.

Pan County was taking advantage of reform and opening up to further engage in comprehensive opening up, rather than being the single-industry as before. Opportunities also followed, in 2013, Pan County transformed into Panzhou City. In 2015, expressways connected every county in Guizhou. Today, the high-speed railway from Shanghai to Kunming has also set up a stop in Panzhou, greatly facilitating the travel of local people. As more and more people enter here, we soon find that there is not only rich coal resources here, but also unique "treasure"!

This "treasure" is the ancient ginkgo tree in Tuole Village, Shiqiao Town, Panzhou. There are 1,000 ancient ginkgo trees in this small village alone.

The first time I heard that number, it startled me.

Sixty years ago, I was a student at Xuhui Middle School in Shanghai. A ginkgo tree was planted not far from the school gate. A naughty student who climbed a tree to break off a twig was not only reprimanded by the head teacher, but also criticized on the school radio. The student was so embarrassed that he couldn't hold up his head for several months, which caused the whole school to be abuzz with discussion.

# Golden

## Tuole Village

情在贵州山水间

1

In Guizhou Province, where I've had a connection for 55 years, there is a young city — Liupanshui City.

I said that Liupanshui City is young, because I remembered very clearly, in 1978 the Liupanshui area was changed to Liupanshui City. That year I was still an educated youth and had not yet left the countryside.

As early as the 1970s, we were very concerned about the news of the Liupanshui area. We had heard that here was rich in high-quality coal mines, a lot of coal dug out in the open pile, too late to transport out, there was a situation of coal spontaneous combustion. What a waste!

Later, it was heard that there were iron ore in Liuzhi and Shuicheng near Pan County, so the government decided to use local coal and iron ore to build steel plants to digest coal and iron ore on the spot. For this purpose, specially Liuzhi, Pan County, Shuicheng as the main city, the Liupanshui area. In the late 1970s, the Liupanshui area was renamed Liupanshui City.

will tell you that the water has gone into the underground river, it doesn't matter, and would remerge from a cave somewhere and flow back into the river.

Which is a river?

Nanpan River, Beipan River, Wu River, and the Duliu River! If you look carefully, the water of the Duliu River and the Nanpan River and Beipan River will eventually flow into the Pearl River, the third largest water system in our country. The Wu River flows directly into the upper reaches of the Yangtze River.

What disconnected from the water in the mountains of Guizhou is the Yellow River. An interesting fact, however, is that the Miao and Buyi villagers in the mountains of Guizhou said firmly that their ancestors originally settled in the Yellow River basin and were the indigenous people there. Only times change, they moved to the mountains...

That's the theme of another short article. To sum up, combined with the ethnic groups living in Guizhou's mountains and rivers, it is actually able to find a lot of topics to say.

heavier, it fell on people's faces so softly that people hardly felt it.

At that period, I kept a diary, and because of that particular time, I could only keep a meteorological diary. All day long in my head thinking about how to describe the rain that falls every day.

The rain fell on the mountains and formed streams in the gullies; The water flowed down the hillside and gradually formed a stream in the village. The water in the stream was almost silent on a clear day, and it can reflect the blue sky and white clouds, reflecting the surrounding mountains. Only when the rain was heavy that the water in the stream made a noise, a rumbling, clattering noise.

If the sound of running water sounded halfway up the mountain, it must be a mountain spring. The mountain cascaded down into a waterfall. It's so spectacular. The rumbling sound seemed to roll down from a distance, hit the cliff wall straight down, that was the waterfall. The most famous waterfalls in Guizhou are Huangguoshu Waterfall and Chishui Waterfall, which originally called Shizhangdong.

Waterfalls, springs, streams, rivers, and rivers are all related to the mountainous area of Guizhou, to its climate, its special karst topography, karst caves and underground rivers in the mountains. These underground river are also one of wonderful scenes in the Guizhou mountains. In a remote mountain village, when you walking along the stream unconsciously, you might suddenly find that the stream disappears. Look around, you will not know where the stream goes. Every time at this time, the local people familiarize myself with the farming tasks, roads, ditches, and endless mountains that could not be seen to the side, as my fellow villagers participated in collective labor. It was funny how many times I tried to count the mountains from a higher place, but after several attempts I realized that it was futile to count the number of mountains where I lived, because the light looked out in one direction and kept on the edge of the mountains beyond the reach of the eye, and the shadows of the mountains were still visible under the sun. At this time, I really realized the true meaning of the phrase the mountains are as numerous as the sea.

In those years, if anyone mentioned Guizhou, they would blurt out: "Sunny days are never more than three days in a row."

Intellectuals say this, workers say this, even officials say this. People with or without culture in the alley say so. In fact, when ten people say this, nine of them have not been to Guizhou, It's just too easy to impress, to sound so rhymed: Sunny days are never more than three days in a row, and the ground is no more than three feet flat.

Later, after living in Guizhou mountain villages for a long time, I really appreciated relationship between Guizhou mountains and water. In addition to God likes rain, heavy rain, thunderstorms, drizzle scattered with the wind, and the kind of "long foot rain" that the villagers spoke of, it seems to fall not big nor small, neither fast nor slow, which is with the wind in the valley, floating over and over, cool and wet. People thought it would stop when it was still falling. People feel it was getting

# Ye Xin

## Wrote Guizhou Landscape

情在贵州山水间

On April 2, 1969, when the sky was getting dark, 800 Shanghai men and women educated youth and I arrived at the small Guiding railway station by train. The radio informed 462 of us who would go to Xiuwen County to get off the train, and after a simple meal of pancake to satisfy our hunger, we moved into the classroom of Guiding Middle School.

When I stood in line all the way into Guiding Middle School in the dark, I only felt that the county was surrounded by mountains. At night, lying on the bunk with the desks and chairs, I felt myself sleepily sleeping in the arms of the mountain. At the night of April 3, we spent the night on the second floor of a thatched-roofed hostel on the cross street of Jiuchang People's Commune. On April 4, after taking a truck for another distance, we walked along the mountain path to the stockade where I had settled down.

The journey made me feel rushed, anxious, and bumpy, with no time or mood to carefully observe everything in the mountainous countryside. It was not until I settled down in this village called Shaguo Village that I began to seriously

Love in the Mountains and Rivers of Guizhou

Xiaoqikong Bridge

moon; gaze a thousand miles, ask who among us can restore rivers and mountains.

I sat down next to the couplet and thought about it: After the Opium War, during the so-called "Five Treaty Ports" period, the Chinese people, under the threat of foreign wars, signed a series of unequal treaties, and the people had no livelihood... In such a turbulent situation, Zhang Zhidong has set up various academies, leaving a widely spread "Jiayou culture", its significance is far more thought-provoking than this incident.

"Jiayou! Jiayou!" It's not something we chant out of habit at events and competitions, it's a call to truly put in the hardwork, to set up and make a real impact!

With that, he opened the lid of the bucket. The bucket was not filled with oil, but some sesame candy, peanut cake, biscuits, walnut cakes and other snacks. I laughed and said, "No lamp oil, it's dessert!"

A man dressed as an official smiled and told me that the story of Zhang Zhidong encouraging the people of Xingyi to add lamp oil is well-known in our area. This is home time for the surrounding primary and secondary schools, we come to the dike at this time every day, one is to remind the playful children to go home early to do homework, to send them snacks; Secondly, Zhaodi National Wetland Park is a 4A level scenic spot. At this time, it is also the time when tourists come most. When they see our dress in the late Qing Dynasty, foreign tourists will ask us what happened, and we just publicize the "Jiayou culture".

What a "Jiayou culture!"

So, one side of the local immediately interjected, "Encourage for themselves, encourage for others, encourage for the cause that is engaged in, is also needed today!"

At that time, I thought of the little grandson of the old classmates in Shanghai, the source of "Jiayou", it was here!

Meanwhile, the significance of the "Jiayou culture" in Anlong County of Xingyi Prefecture is not only to answer the source of the two words "Jiayou", but also has far-reaching significance.

That is when I passed the half mountain pavilion and saw a pair of couplets on the pavilion column, I thought of it. The couplets read: Bring a pot of wine, to talk about the wind and subordinate counties of Xingyi Prefecture.

In order to encourage the children of poor families to study, study hard, and think deeply, he ordered the small officials in the government to carry a load of lamp oil and go around in the streets and alleys of Xingyi City (today's Anlong County town) at night. Whenever they saw who is still lit at home, they would knock on the door and enter the house, if they found someone in the house reading at night, the small officals would refill lamp oil, in order to encourage the students to stay up at night to read, do not worry about the lamp oil will burn out.

The story of the governor adding lamp oil to encourage students spread one after another. At one time, it was a good story among the people, and it also became the motivation for parents to encourage their children to read. The trend of studying hard has spread throughout urban and rural areas, and for a time, in Anlong and other counties of Xingyi Prefecture, there has been an unprecedented flourishing learning scene. Especially children from poor farming families, it is a tradition to stay up all night to read. Those from wealthy families, not to mention. "The book has its own golden house", reading was way for them to win fame and fortune in the future!

When I was walking along Anlong's famous lotus pond, on the sloping embankment at sunset, I met two levee guards dressed in Qing Dynasty official clothes, one of them carrying a load and one of them carrying an oil spoon in his hand. I couldn't help laughing and asked, "Why? Do we still need to add lamp oil to the pupils' homes?"

grandfather and grandson, "Jiayou, Jiayou! I have shouted all my life, but I really don't know why."

Unexpectedly, in this year's New Year's Day, I was invited to Guizhou Qianxinan prefecture, when I visited Anlong County at the border where Guizhou, Guangxi, Yunnan three provinces meet, I obtained the answer to this question.

I've been to Anlong County many times. It is known that this county with a population of nearly 500,000, which belongs to a small county in Guizhou and the whole country, is one of the first named historical and cultural cities. Humans have been here for more than 10,000 years. Absolutely did not expect that it was such a place, but it was the first mountain where "Jiayou" was shouted out.

The words have to start from Zhang Zhidong, one of the four most important ministers in the late Qing Dynasty. In 1841, Zhang's father, Zhang Ying, was appointed governor of Xingyi Prefecture. Zhang Ying is not only an official, but also an intellectual with thought, pursuit and ambition. Coming to this remote border of Guizhou, Guangxi and Yunnan Provinces, he continued to reinvigorate education as he had done when he was an official elsewhere. He believed that in order to revitalize China, revive the great cause, and let China get rid of poverty and weakness, talents were the first thing. And to foster talents, we must develop education. In Xingyi Prefecture (Anlong), he founded the Xingyi Prefecture Trial Institute, rebuilt Zhuquan Academy, and "persuaded and donated" the Ceheng Academy and the Panshui Academy in Puan. Shiheng and Puan were all

# Jiayou and Anlong

情在贵州山水间

In the fall, I accompanied an old friend to the kindergarten to pick up his grandson.

There is a tug of war in the kindergarten, a sound of encouragement "Jiayou" "Jiayou" shouted out from the children's mouth, it appears clear and pleasant, filled the small playground with excitement. (notation: jiayou means encourage.)

When he picked up his grandson and walked out of the spacious lane, the little boy suddenly asked his grandfather a question, "When the tug of war, why do everyone call 'Jiayou'?"

My old friend who have been together for 60 years could not answer for a moment, turned around, transfer this question to me, and said, "Grandpa can not answer. You can ask grandpa Ye, he writes books."

The little guy immediately raised his face to me, his black eyes were wide open, and he asked me, "Grandpa Ye, do you know?"

I had to honestly spread out my hands and said to the

the original custom, that is, on this day, the daughters and son-in-law will go to the home of their parents, while visiting the elderly with their grandchildren, they will clean the quilt for their parents, and send a new set of clothes for their parents to bring holiday joy.

I thought to myself: When the old Buyi people of Libo enjoy this new custom, they will also have a kind of intoxicated happiness as I do when I hear the song of the Buyi girl.

of applause and shouts, as the guests who had come to see the Double Six Festival shouted:

"Sing it again, it's wonderful!"

"Sing in Mandarin that we understand. We want to know what you're singing."

The Buyi girl shyly took a look at the accompaniment guy, and as soon as the music was played, the girl sang in her unique Mandarin, "You are in the corn forest on the slope, did you hear the good voice? You don't need to answer, just know my heart."

Buyi girl's Mandarin was not very standard, but she could enunciate clearly, most people understand, and people respond with bursts of cheers and applause. I only thought that the lyrics were obviously improvised, general, but by her voice singing, a girl in love with the heart, suddenly let people feel. This is the true sound of nature.

When people clamored for her to sing again, a large group of Buyi men and women gathered around her, and immediately submerged her in the ocean of joy of the Double Six Festival. Gongs, drums and Suona sounded one after another, and the smiling faces of men and women shook in front of my eyes. But I was still immersed in the song of Buyi girl, that sweet with magnetic and glutinous voice, echoed in my heart again and again, like an ancient echo, like a girl's heart call and true feelings, instantly I had a drunk feeling.

With the improvement of Libo Buyi people's life, today's Double Six Festival has added a new content that was not in groups is that there are few words such as love and missing in the songs, and they are not like many folk songs with a kind of provocative fun meaning, but more use of "bixing" and "metaphor" to let the listener experience and taste.

The Libo's Buyi love song is similar, which is soft and graceful, lively and short. As a person savor one line, a new sentence comes again. There is no introduction and no liner, the lyrics are often improvised.

The Buyi girl singing in front of me was wearing a simple dress with a tight cut, with only a few small flowers embroidered on the front and sleeve. As soon as the music was played, her left hand naturally raised to one side, and her voice was bright, and she sang it in Buyi, and as soon as she sang a sentence, the clear and bright voice like a spring in the mountains attracted a burst of applause and applause from the onlookers: awesome!

When she sang the second line, no one clapped and shouted anymore, they were captivated. Although I could not understand a word of Buyi's language, my eyes, with her singing, turned into a picture of a couple in the drizzle: a couple holding a flower umbrella and walking beside a bamboo forest; Romeo and Juliet talking on a balcony; in the moonlight by the river, men and women were whispering as if no one were watching...

The singing was sweet and pleasant, transmitting a waxy and tender emotion that the singers in other places do not have, which made the soft singing add a trembling taste.

What did it feel like?

My thoughts were interrupted by a more intense round

the hearts of both sides understand that the song carries their yearning for love, with intentional investigation and questioning, expressing their yearning and pursuit of a better life. Heart-to-heart young men and women, in this process, deeply in love with each other, or private engagement for life.

Therefore, in the Double Six Festival, people eat the best wine and dinner, young men and women wear national costumes that fully show their handsome and beautiful.

The recognized top three "Song Kings" selected every year in the Double Six Festival will be admired and supported by all Buyi people, and every family will invite the "song King" to sing in their own courtyard or house, so that the villagers in the village will come to learn and enjoy. This encourages younger men and women to compete to be the "King of Song" in the coming year.

When the singing is in full swing, the celebration can go on all night, with no one leaving. I am not good at drinking, the reason why I want to write this article is that I unconsciously drunk when I listened to the Buyi girl singing the song, and I felt more enjoy than drinking the old Moutai.

Come to think of it, I am over seventy years old, and I have heard many singers, male and female, including the king of the world singers, but I still feel a sense of intoxication when I listen to the songs of Buyi girls. Shouldn't such a Buyi folk love song be written down in words?

The biggest difference between the love songs of Buyi girls and the love songs of young men and women of other ethnic described such a Buyi cottage, understanding of educated youth is superficial.

This brings me to the title of this article: *Drunk Song*.

Not singing after drunk, nor drunk listening to people singing, but listening to those touching songs, intoxicated with the kind of feeling of flying among clouds.

The Buyi in Libo, like the Buyi scattered in Qiannan and all over the province, celebrate Double Six Festival, which is the sixth day of the sixth month of the Chinese calendar. On this day, in addition to the New Year, the Dragon Boat customs, such as killing pigs and sheep, drinking together, there is a unique tradition: connecting with others and expressing emotions through songs. Double Six Festival, that's how it came about. Middle-aged and elderly Buyi people, in the song festival to talk about family affection, while drinking wine, while singing big songs. The big songs appear the history of Buyi people, folklore and mythology, if there are foreign guests, they will greet you to drink rice wine, while singing to you the origin of Double Six Festival. This song has a narrative nature, so the melody is soft and soothing, leisurely to give you the message. This kind of singing is also called "wine song", drinking wine, singing, listening, in this atmosphere, unconsciously, the host and guests will be immersed in it, the body and mind have a wonderful feeling with tipsy. And young men and women, sing lively, bright small songs. Small song is the most favorite form of young men and girls, who use them to express their talent, singing out their heart's true feelings to a specific person they love. Only

103

# Drunk Song

## of Double Six Festival

情在贵州山水间

In my novel "Five Sisters", Geng Zhuang, a young Buyi man who could catch fish, sing and love to drink, trembled educated youth Sha Haihong's heart with his unique and beautiful singing voice. She was attracted by him unconsciously and later married Geng Zhuang. Sha Haihong's fate as a female educated youth has twists and turns.

Readers with the same educated youth experience, especially those who also educated in ethnic minority villages, criticized me, saying that the singing of ethnic minority young men and women is indeed good, but it only sounds good when they hear it. It is impossible to sing Sha Haihong so distraught that she ended up marrying him, as I have described. The reason why there is such a story plot is for the needs of the novel I made up. Educated youth also heckled me to tell the truth, is it not so.

I can only say that although many educated youth have come into contact with ethnic minorities who are good at singing and dancing in the countryside, and some educated youth can even sing and dance, they do not really have a deep understanding of ethnic minority song and dance culture. Specific to the village I change with the light and shadow of the four seasons, giving people a sense of colorful each other. One moment the water was dark green, the next a lighter blue, the next a deep blue...

What is the reason?

Libo, a typical karst landscape, is covered with layers of virgin forest. Lush forests need abundant water to nourish, and large areas of forests with its selfless conservation of water sources, play a role in soil and water conservation. On the contrary, the water is surprisingly clear and bright. Similarly, in the carbonate rocks of the mountain, calcium carbonate and magnesium carbonate dissolve into the water, forming a large number of free calcium ions and magnesium ions, making the water color change a variety of colorful scenery that we are pleased to see.

Oh, people call Wolong Pool a colorful lake, it turns out there is a reason, a basis.

The waters of Libo are inexhaustible.

The multicolor of water in Xiaoqikong is just more concentrated.

In fact, deep into the river hinterland of Libo, you can also find more fascinating water colors.

pairs of mandarin ducks playing together intimately; Second, a thousand years old Mandarin Duck Trees in the lake stand side by side and accompanies each other; Third, the fish in the lake, including huge carp, and rare copper fish — small and pointed head, small eyes, mouth in the next place. I have been to Yuanyang Lake several times, focusing on the color of the water.

Especially on a sunny day, the color of the lake changes when the sun rises; When the hot sun is in the sky, the lake is a golden and silver color; As the sun set in the west, the lake changed into other attractive colors. Look, the evergreen trees around the Yuanyang Lake are reflected in it, with the sun shining from different angles on the sparkling lake, the lake is sometimes sapphire crystal bright, sometimes agate color, sometimes like lilac, black rose, emerald color, give me the feeling of colorful dazzling, no wonder Yuanyang Lake is also known as Yao pool, said it is comparable to the fairyland in the sky.

The same scenic spot to enjoy the colorful water is the last Wolong Pool in Xiaoqikong scenic spot.

The water of Wolong Pool catches the eye with the huge silver curtain that plummets down. Tourists often flock to take pictures in front of the huge water from the river. Up and down, left and right, people stand in various poses and cheer for photos. Crowded people, after photography, they feel that the job is done, often neglect to appreciate the gorgeous beauty of the pool.

The seemingly calm Wolong Pool water there will also

Holding onto a tree trunk, I turned half way around and called out to my wife, who was not in the water, to take a picture of the tree, the stone and the water. As I stood to take the picture, a thought came to my mind:

The tree I held tightly in my hand, soaked in water all year round, grew so strong, why not be drowned by the cold water?

The tour guide on the shore with a megaphone, as if reading my mind, answered the question. She said that according to scientists, as the water flows in the river, the carbon dioxide in the water is deposited and the calcium carbonate is deposited, which covers the ground in the river. At the same time, the plant roots are tightly wrapped, forming a protective calcification layer.

The secret of not drowning the trees in the Aquatic forest, turns out to be here.

This is really a mysterious side of nature that we rarely see.

What makes me think of the title of "Multicolor of Water" is Yuanyang Lake, one of the most photographed and famous scenic spots in Xiaoqikong.

It's the name of Yuanyang Lake. Are couples willing to flock here?

Not also, Yuanyang Lake is not a favorite among young lovers, all the year round, no matter what season, into Xiaoqikong scenic area, by Yuanyang Lake, there are always boats on the lake, the lake shore is always crowded, full of tourists of all ages, everyone standing in their chosen position, competing for photography.

Boating on the Yuanyang Lake offer three sights: First,

情在贵州山水间

I was attracted by the surprisingly clear and bright color of the water in the water forest, and resolutely entered the Aquatic forest with bare feet. In the official summer season, the Shanghai partners in the same company pulled their trouser legs up high. Sun, who took the lead in stepping into the water, first cheered,

"It's so comfortable, come down, all come down!"

He encouraged us with a smile on his face and an expression of satisfaction.

Sun is three years older than me, he dares to go down, I can not go down?

When my feet stepped into the knee−deep clear water of Aquatic forest, the first feeling is exciting, deep cold, in the hot summer is able to bear the cold, and a kind of comfortable, so it's instant for me to adapt.

Led by Sun and me, our companions walked into the Aquatic forest one after another. Oh, it was the happiest I've ever had, the happiest I've ever felt, seeing the bright, clear water flowing between our feet. On the rocks of the river−bed, I saw numerous trees growing−oaks, hollies, maples Chinese bishopwoods and other trees whose names I can't name, all with their roots firmly planted in the rock beneath the water. Looking down, the root system went through the rock and took root in the river bed below the stone, forming a landscape with stones in the water, trees in the cracks between the stones, and trees growing in the water. Grasping a tree trunk, I shook it a few times, but the tree was motionless. I have never seen such a wonderful sight of water, stone and trees clinging to each other.

98

bay, I saw the unusual Laya waterfall, like an avalanche pouring down. Instead of the shape and gentle style in my memory, the water crashed onto the road, occupying more than half of the land for tourists to walk and watch.

In order to commemorate Emei's sacrifice to save the villagers and remember her forever, the Buyi people named the cascading waterfall Laya Waterfall, so that all friends in the world can see this waterfall and think of this beautiful Buyi girl.

Today, when more and more Chinese and foreign tourists walk into the Xiaoqikong Scenic area and see Laya Waterfall, amazed at her gentle beauty, they should also know this sad and touching story that I heard in Buyi Village in my youth.

If Laya waterfall is a beautiful myth, then, located in the upper reaches of the Xiangshui River peak cluster depression, surrounded by green mountains and green valleys. The fields are full of green valley waterfalls, it is more like a small jasper, only to see more than 60 meters of green bushes, like a jade belt attached to the green wall along the mountain, the mountain appears more green, the water becomes whiter, more unhurried sense of agility. Next to the splashing water, floating gauzy mist, it will be more shocking to see, and tourists will wake up after a long while to take pictures to commemorate.

If it is said that the 68-level waterfall, Laya waterfall, Cuigu waterfall in Xiaoqikong scenic area each has its own form, each has its own color. Then, where you are into Aquatic forest, pull up pants, take off shoes and socks, you can experience the world's rare feelings, experience the thrill of water singing.

noise, congestion and laughter of the tide of tourists, completely ignoring the accompaniment of the ringing water river. There are also tourists, attracted by the ever-changing water colors of the Galactic waterfall, to enjoy the different forms of the water scene, up and down the 68-level waterfall, wandering several back and forth, still do not want to leave.

When people are tired of walking, they choose what they think is the perfect position, sit down, and still enjoy with their eyes wide open.

Is there any other waterfall in the world that can be so charming?

If the 68-level waterfall is wonderful in lying there for people to enjoy, then the Laya Waterfall in Xiaoqikong scenic area, people can not help but admire it at first glance, "Oh, the waterfall is like a beautiful woman!"

Her beautiful and elegant appearance is like a beautiful woman after a bath with a white veil.

In Buyi's language, "Laya" just means "beautiful maiden." So most people feel the same way Buyi did when he named it.

But I happen to have seen a different face of the "pretty girl".

In the early summer of 2011, it was Libo spring flood, the waves of the few days, I entered Xiaoqikong scenic area, had not gone to Laya waterfall to catch a glimpse of the girl's beauty, only to hear the rumble of thunder in the distance, the whole situation was a landslide, I quickly turned around the mountain along the Xiangshui Valley, from the bottom up to the gentle slope to the height of 1.6 kilometers, and then walk back, top−down review, take photos at each position, shooting from every angle, take endless beauty, and make a smile again and again. Some people say, where are there 68 levels of water? I counted, only 57 levels. Someone immediately refuted. You do not count carefully, I count in the heart, every ups and downs, there are more than seventy or eighty levels. Others laughed, "Why is it level 68?"

It is the Buyi and Yao people who have lived here for generations. They like the lucky numbers 6 and 8, and use this long waterfall to symbolize their good wishes. They pray that their days on earth will always flow like the flowing water of the Xiangshui River all year round. I wish their life will always be as lush and evergreen as the green mountains on both sides of the Xiangshui River, with auspicious seasons.

In the valley of the Xiangshui River, beautiful and eager music is played day and night, sometimes soothing and elegant, sometimes wild. The white surface of the water is sometimes wide and sometimes narrow, and the color of the water changes from green to blue; The drops splashed from the waterfalls are as large as magnolia, small as pearl jade, crystal clear, jumping like a dance in general. Early in the morning and at dusk, the river valley is filled with beautiful fog gauze, appearing white and blue, photographers will lean down to occupy the terrain of the river bank, and press the shutter absorbedly, capturing the dreamlike scenery in the water mist, completely ignoring the

# Multicolor
## of water

情在贵州山水间

The multicolor water is arguably the biggest and most attractive feature of Libo.

And to see this feature, we must enter Xiaoqikong scenic spot.

This may also explain why, since Libo was rated as the highest honor of bing a World Natural Heritage site, the guests who flocked to visit the Xiaoqikong scenic spot accounted for ninety percent.

The variety of water is so eye-catching.

The color of the water is so mysterious and seductive.

The water evokes the imagination. So that when people come back from Libo and ask him what they remember most, he will say waterfall. The view of the waterfall is so beautiful and unforgettable.

And the most memorable, is the 68-level waterfall.

Other waterfalls are from high mountains flying down, and the 68-level waterfall, lying in the river valley toward you, pushing the snow and jade general spray toward people, astonishing everyone who sees it. Some people have counted, they want to be good with each other. At our age, people don't care if they can."

"Cross—ethnic marriage! There are not only Shui and Buyi married, capable handsome, a little skilled Buyi, Shui young men, but also married beautiful girls from other provinces back to the cottage!" The village cadre gave me a supplementary introduction on the side, and then he gave me a finger count, a count of five or six provinces. Saying this, he laughed, "These Han girls, married to the village, are enterprising! They learn from our Shui people to make wine, learn Buyi batik, saying they will turn it into to city—style drinks and clothing. With fate, every nation can become a family!"

For me, this is the biggest gain I've had in years. I am more and more clearly aware that the ethnic marriage customs and inter—ethnic marriage that I was familiar with and understood about the specific procedures 40 or 50 years ago, with the development of the times and the impact of the wage wave, generations of young men and girls of all ages have flooded into the city, and are undergoing subtle and quite obvious changes. At this point, even the elderly ethnic minorities in remote villages, who are older than me, will point their heads and admit, "The world has changed. People's feelings and customs have changed imperceptibly!"

Should love?

It's not a problem.

Today, the young generation of Libo ethnic mixed place, proves this with their life experience.

93

community's holiday is also to celebrate. The more opportunities for contact, the more times of "eye to eye", just as they sing in their popular song:

**You look at me,**
**I look at you,**
**Right on we fall in love with each other...**

There are people of the same lineage marry each other, and there are people of different races marry each other. So, will it still be like the situation I interviewed decades ago, which is considered to violate the rules of the family, violate the ancestral teachings, and cause trouble?

No, no, no.

Older parents, whether they are Buyi, Shui or Miao, will say to me in a positive tone, "The key is the two youths themselves, just like each other. We don't care."

The mother of a Buyi girl, a woman nearly fifty years old, said to me, "No matter which one she marries, as long as she is willing to live a happy life by labor, I will accept it, and at most tell her a few words about how to be a wife."

The mother of another aquarium girl in her early 40s looked at her husband and said frankly with a smile, "They young people say about 'sparks'– if they feel sparks for each other, who can stop it?"

Her husband added while smoking, "Shui, Buyi, Miao, Dong, put on work clothes to head into the city, leave us so far,

at me, "No! Mr. Ye. People get married and have families."
Some village men and women frankly said to me, "Now all go to work in large and medium—sized cities, many customs have changed.We do this symbolically only when we return to our elders, so that they will be happy."

The traditional "blind date", "matchmaking", "engagement", "date booking" and other cumbersome rituals have also been simplified.

Libo County in Guizhou is an ethnic county, with the minority population accounting for more than 92%. In many places, Buyi, Shui, Miao, Yao ethnic are the main. In the national festival in Libo, I often see that the Shui people celebrate the Mao Festival, and the young people of Buyi, Yao, Miao, and Zhuang ethnic people living in eight villages in four townships will wear their distinctive costumes and come to participate in them cheerfully. They also laugh, sing and dance, like their own festival. On the contrary, the Buyi people celebrate the June Double Six Festival, the Yao people celebrate the Tuoluo Festival, the Panwang Festival, the Miao people celebrate the Lusheng Festival, and other ethnic people also come to participate. Not only young men and women rushed to participate in the festival activities, but also elders also love to take advantage of the festival, go to the village, to their friends of the other ethnic family to drink wine, heart to heart, play a happy. The unmarried boys and girls sing and dance freely, taking advantage of this opportunity to find their partner.

Your community's holiday is like this, and our

pouring the water into the water tank, while chatting with the host family, exchanging pleasantries, through this process, but also enhance mutual understanding. More than 30 years ago, in the 1980s, this tradition was extremely common.

Today, the new wives have told me that it is already over, "Mr. Ye, you don't know it? Water pipes into every household, there is no need for new bride to carry water!"

Those words woke me up!

Following this line of thinking, and carefully communicating with them in ethnic villages, I suddenly found that those customs, slangs, manners, rules, and procedures that I had previously assumed to be immutable were also quietly and imperceptibly evolving under the impact of the tide of the times, just like "a new wife carrying water."

Among the ethnic minorities living in Guizhou, on the night of marriage, there is a tradition called "not to stay in the husband's home", that is, the bride does not sleep with the groom, but is accompanied by the bridesmaids to sleep, after one night (or three nights), they return to the mother's home, separated for a few days, the groom brings gifts, then goes to the home, visits the in-laws, and then brings the bride back to complete the marriage. That's when the wedding is over.

There are differences in specific details; The bride has a long time to live in her mother's home, but the traditional practice of "not returning to her husband's home" and "returning to the door" is still a necessary procedure. Is that still the custom?

Some young girls and daughters-in-law waved their hands

marriage and unity. The novel "By the Green River" is written about this theme.

I have always believed that customs of the ethnic minority love, marriage ethnics, are handed down from ancient times, adhere to thousands of years of tradition, will not change.

Like waking up from a dream, over the years, I went back to Guizhou every year, had time to go deep into the Miao, Dong, Buyi villages, and was often invited to participate in ethnic minority festivals with great interest: the Mao festival and Duan festival of the Shui ethnic, the Guzang Festival of the Miao ethnic, the June 6 of Buyi, and the lively wedding.

I sat at the guest table, drinking rice wine, quietly observing the etiquette of the ethnic minorities to worship the elderly, listening to their joyful songs, looking at their costumes, and sometimes left the table to join them in the dance. I could not help noticing that the rules and procedures which I had thought immutable were different from those which I had seen half a century before.

For example, there is a tradition in the marriage customs of the Buyei ethnic that on the few days when the bride officially settled in her husband's family, she would not only meet with her husband the relatives on the left and right houses and the village, especially the elders, but also carry water for the relatives and elders living in the village early in the morning, and fill the water tanks of their families. Firstly, it allows the husband's family to see if the bride is diligent and capable of labor. Secondly, the cool water is picked into the homes of relatives and elders, while

# Should We Love?

情在贵州山水间

I'm asking myself and others.

Should we love?

Such questions are often raised when it comes to minority marriages.

More than 50 years ago, when I first came to Guizhou and met the ethnic minorities living in the mountain villages, I touched on this topic when I communicated with them for writing inspiration. And will be told, whether it is Miao, Buyi, Dong, Yi ethnic, or Shui, Tujia, Gelao ethnic, they insist on the same ethnic group in marriage, interethnic marriage is rare or even not allowed. When a Han young man and a minority girl fall in love, they more or less have to go through some twists and turns before they can get married. Between ethnic minorities, when they fall in love and propose to get married, it often causes discussions between the two ethnics. In the specific operating procedures and wedding etiquette, disputes will be caused. Especially in remote places, conflicts arise from disagreements and the stubbornness of both sides, and even break up in discord.

I have also written works on such subject, involving

Shenlong River source. But after the long rope, the stone did not sink to the bottom. Second, there is a strange phenomenon in the Shenlong River. If the weather is clear for a long time without rain, the water of the Shenlong River will rise, and it will soon overflow the river edge, and it will rain; When the weather is not clear for a long time, the Shenlong River water will ebb tide, the less the river receded, the lower the surface the fall, and the day will be open and clear when it is about to see the river bed. Remarkably, through both rise and fall, the water remains crystal clear and sweet to drink, cherished by Tujia people as their life source.

I walked along the stone steps of the Shenlong River, walked to the stockade near 800 meters, I saw the river flowing into a gap that looked like a ditch, strange! The river ran away and disappeared. Where did it go? Oh, the shortest river on earth. What a magical river.

情在贵州山水间

I made up my mind to spare three days, not only climbed Fanjing Mountain to admire the landscape on the peak, saw the dove like davidia flowers in the clean valley of thousand mountains, but finally walked to the shortest river in the world — Shenlong River.

Without walking to the river, it is hard to imagine that there really is such a short river in the world. Local Tujia villagers told me that the river is only one and a half miles long. I pulled the rope to measure, and it was 750 — 800 meters. Less than a kilometer.

Is there a shorter river in the world?

This place is called Cloud House. In Tujia, it means "the place where monkeys drink water". It was dusk, and the setting sun sprinkled the clear water of the Shenlong River with countless gold and silver spots. There were Tujia women, talking and laughing, washing green vegetables in the small weir from the river. At the source, a young man was leaning over to carry water. In the Tujia village, smoke rose from the chimneys, the sound of chicken and dogs filled the air. Outside the village, the fields and fields are scattered, and the lush trees spread out to the mountain called Mercury Slope there, which is really a good scenery of the Shenlong River.

Tujia villagers say that this river, the shortest in the world, has two other wonders. First, the river is unfathomable, slack season, there have been more than 30 young men, each took out a basket of ropes to connect into a long rope, rope head tied to a large stone, sunk into the pool, want to measure the depth of the

Hunan Province and Yuping in Guizhou Province, there were always passengers on the train who said that they could get off here and drive for half a day to reach Fanjing Mountain. But only heard people say, never see people really get off to visit Fanjing Mountain.

After I went from being a educated youth to a writer, I started to work in Guiyang, a provincial city and traveled all over the province, but I never visited Fanjing Mountain. In those days, to Tongren, where Fanjing Mountain is located, I had to take a two-day bus and stay one night in a small hotel in the mountainous countryside. It's a four-day round trip. At the foot of the mountain, climbing up Fanjing Mountain up and down took an additional three days. It is difficult to get Tongren once in your life, you can't just climb a mountain, you have to take a look at the city, you have to turn around other landscapes, you have to meet with friends of the Literary Federation and the Writers Association to talk about a little work, and you can't get out of it if you don't prepare to spend 10 days. At that time, I still had some duties in the provincial city, and it was impossible for me to leave my work and go out for a full 10 days. So although I have lived and worked in Guizhou for 21 years, I have never been to Fanjing Mountain. The shortest Shenlong River in the world is naturally talked about by people as miraculous, rather than witnessed.

Now well, with most of the highways built from Guiyang to Tongren, through the high speed, it takes almost five hours by car to reach Fanjing Mountain.

# The Shortest

**River on Earth in Legend**

情在贵州山水间

The shortest river on earth, rumored to be unique and magical, but inaccessible.

Local villagers also call it the shortest river in the world, everyone can glance from the source of the river to the disappearance of the river, the villagers named it Shenlong River.

The Shenlong River lies at the foot of Fanjing Mountain, where Guizhou and Hunan Provinces meet. To say that it is not easy to reach is my personal experience. Fanjing Mountain is a famous Buddhist mountain, more than 40 years ago to Guizhou to settle down, I heard the reputation of Fanjing Mountain. It is said that there is a kind of flower on this mountain, rarely seen in the world, when in full bloom, it is like a white dove spreading its wings to fly; It is said that there is a stone on this mountain, which some people call a book of a thousand pages, others say a book of ten thousand volumes, in a word, just like thousands of books stacked together, which will never topple; Only, it is on the Golden Peak, ten times climbed up, nine times can not see its true face. Once you encounter it, once you see it, your luck is in.

At that time, when I took the train to pass Xinhuang in

84

I said, "No, no, I am visiting the old place, these scenic spots can be detailed naturally." In fact, I know that in addition to the "Hongyun Golden Peak", there is a "Old Golden Peak", I want him to seize the time to see the rare snow in the Fanjing Mountain.

Really, when we moved from the "new Jinding" to the north along the ridge, the terrain was high and open, the vision was wide, the forest sea, the rolling clouds and waves of the "Old Golden Peak", were all enveloped in a snow fog, the famous "Ten Thousand Books" as if they were carefully framed into snow-white and thickened "silver book" classics. In the past many times to see the "flip sky print" also changed its appearance. Even the two natural round pits, "gold box" and "jade stove", also appeared more magical and attractive.

I also wanted to see the "One-line sky" and "Jade Emperor's roof", Li pointed to the sky and said, "Don't go, Mr. Ye, you are 75 years old, I still have to be responsible for your safety!"

Of course I had to obey him! But I asked one thing, "Don't say a word, and let me stand still for a few minutes on the Old Golden Peak."

Chief Li shut his mouth at that time and stared at me uncomprehending. I had no explanation. Only, I clearly heard the melody of "Fantaisie-Impromptu" again.

That's the melody of Yuntian solo Fanjing Mountain.

major landscapes in Fanjing Mountain, which was blanketed in snow. The "Fanzeng Mountain", which is pure stone and has no soil and is shaped like a huge steamed rice cooker, is covered with snow. Li, the local propaganda section chief accompanying me, reminded me, "Mr. Ye, do you remember? The local villagers and woodsmen used to call this mountain 'Fanzeng Mountain', because there were so many scholars and writers, and because people often entered the mountain and called this place the ancient Buddha dojo, finally named it Fanjing Mountain."

I told Chief Li that when I came to Fanjing Mountain in the early years, one of the literati accompanying me had worked in the village at the foot of the mountain, and he had introduced them to me in detail. "All you have to do," I said, "is show me all the places I usually see when I come here in other seasons."

Under the snow, I really counldn't see clearly. So the chief of Section Li immediately came to the spirit, he promised, "I will get!" Raised his voice and gave me pointers and introductions.

"Here is a pillar of Brahma, the golden sword breaks the gorge. The name of the scenic spot is 'Jindao Gorge'; There are several scenic spots that poet Liao Yunpeng of Yinjiang County at the end of the Qing Dynasty wrote a poem 'iron rope to help people to heaven' to praise: Dingboshi, Guanyindong, Taizishi, Lingguanyan, Tianxianqiao, Sheshenyan... Mr.Ye, am I speaking too fast?" The young section chief Li paused as he spoke, staring at me.

all the old Guizhou will tell me that it will inevitably snow on Fanjing Mountain.

It is also a coincidence that in January 2024, I really waited for this snow. The snow was so heavy that I was desperate to stay in the guest house on Fanjing Mountain before the scenic area was closed. At that time, there were few guests and no one was lonely. When I went to Fanjing Mountain in the quiet snow, I really felt that I had entered a different ice and snow world from the human world. The myriad and extraordinary mountains were all enveloped in a white, which made me sincerely feel that this was a wonderful holy place.

I was looking for "Hongyun Golden Peak", one of the six

and Songtao County. It is not only the tallest mountain in Guizhou, but also the main peak of Wuling Mountain Range. It is a giant standing on the big slope of the transition from Yunnan–Guizhou Plateau to Xiangxi Hills. When I went to Fenghuang in Hunan , it was from Tongren side of the past!

Fanjing, these two words, until today, is still the name of many girls in the surrounding area! When a female baby was born, she was named Lv Fanjing and Ma Fanjing. It can be seen that Fanjing Mountain is really a good name.

In spring, I went to Fanjing Mountain to enjoy the pigeon flowers, the petals of the flowers are larger than the petals of magnolia in Shanghai, fulfilling me with beauty.

In summer, I climbed the Fanjing Mountain, sweating, and then standing on the top of the mountain. No matter where the comfortable mountain wind blowing, my feeling was really beautiful so that I wanted to sing.

In autumn, the flowers on Fanjing Mountain bloomed in the lush green shade, and the fragrance of the flowers dispersed with the wind, always leading me to open my eyes to find where the flowers are.

In winter, I never got the chance to go to Fanjing Mountain. But the friend of the management committee told me that Fanjing Mountain in winter is the most beautiful. When you walk into Fanjing Mountain which is transformed by snow and moon, you can really feel what kind of realm "Fanjing" is. Moreover, whenever I ask where it is most likely to snow in winter in Guizhou Province, which is located in the southwest,

If I tell you that every time I climb to the top of Guizhou Fanjing Mountain, the melody of "Fantaisie—Impromptu" will also sound in my ears along with the wind, you will surely wonder: why do you want to put the famous song and the famous mountain together? It's almost irrelevant.

But for me, this is what happens every time I climb Fanjing Mountain.

Fanjing Mountain is a famous mountain. I have heard from friends of the scenic area management committee that since it was listed on the World Natural Heritage list, every year from early spring to late autumn, 8000 tickets are sold out every day.

As for me, because I have been associated with Guizhou for more than half a century, a total of 55 years, I have climbed the "Golden Peak" and "Ten Thousand Books" of Fanjing Mountain countless times in the front and back mountains.

My friends who have not been to Fanjing Mountain may not know that there are six most famous landscapes on the peak of Fanjing Mountain, of which "Mushroom Stone", "Old Golden Peak" and "Hongyun Golden Peak" are must—go to see the beauty.

When I went to Fanjing Mountain as a young man, I wrote this impressive mountain into my novel. I was afraid that some people would recognize Fanjing Mountain, so I gave it another name: Wulan Mountain. The result was criticized by readers: Fanjing Mountain is so big, what are you afraid of?

Fanjing Mountain is located in Tongren City, Guizhou Province, at the junction of Jiangkou County, Yinjiang County

# Clounds

**Solo on Fanjing Mountain**

情在贵州山水间

Chopin has a piece titled *Fantaisie-Impromptu*, today's performers will perform it with a piano solo, will also play it with a flute to show it, in either form, will let people get artistic enjoyment in a few minutes.

I heard this song more than 50 years ago in a friend's home, and immediately borrowed the record home, and when I read, I turned the sound of the record player down to a low level, listening to it over and over again.

Why? I can't explain it. I read it when I was a child, and my grandchildren still read it, just as everyone remembers the poem "This morn of spring in bed I'm lying, not wake up till I hear birds crying." As to why, I can't explain.

What can be said is that this is a classic of art, enduring and eternal.

It's true of "This morn of spring in bed I'm lying", it's true of "The general was so angry that his hair uplifted his hat,simply for a beautiful concubine", it's true of "A drizzling rain falls like tears on the Mourning Day", and it's certainly true of "Fantaisie-Impromptu".

scenery changes, many guests feel that it is not satisfied as a tourist, choosing—to live down.

Buyi villagers said that it was the enthusiasm of the guests that allowed us to "eat tourist meals" and cross the poverty line.

Today, each guest house is more inviting than the last. The hotel's service and reception facilities are also in line with the world outside the mountain. Out of poverty, the Buyi villagers are happy to use their industrious and intelligent footsteps to walk on the road of revitalizing the countryside.

Wanfenglin is performing a more exciting and pleasing tone.

the fairyland scenery of Wanfenglin, I once again entered a state of silence, for a long time to enjoy the beauty of this piece which was distinct from what we had seen at Huajiang Slope the day before. The heart is accompanied by the rhythm of the music, welling uncontrollable longing.

I said to myself, one day, I must go into the gauze-like clounds of Wanfenglin, to explore the mysterious world of Wanfenglin.

I have been connected with the mountains of Guizhou for more than half a century, a full 55 years. God did not live up to my wishes and yearning, and in the years, I walked into Wanfenglin from far and near, bottom-up and top-down, and explored the landscape of Wanfenglin enough and thoroughly.

It turns out that this is the home of the Buyi people for generations. Rice, fruits and vegetables are grown on the flat dam land between thousands of mountain peaks. On the slate slope next to the mountain road, along the natural undulation of the mountain, a series of Buyi characteristic farmhouses have been built. Generation after generation, Buyi villagers work at sunrise and rest at sunset on the land of Wanfenglin, living a simple and poor peasant life,peacefully and contentedly.

In the years of poverty alleviation, such a large and beautiful Wanfenglin was assessed as a World Natural Heritage, and guests from all over the country and all over the world flocked to see this refreshing beauty.

Landscape is a painting, all the way is a scene. Flowers bloom differently in spring, summer, autumn and winter, the

In front of the towering Huajiang Slope, thousands of mountains and peaks were located unobstructed. All the forests seemed to boil and soar under the bright sun, floating in the mist that curled around the peaks and ridges.

The slope of the Huajiang River is too high, standing on the top of the mountain top of the Huajiang River, the mountain wind whistling, shaking our clothes. We could only hear each other if we shout louder.

Looking at the magnificent scene in front of thousands of mountains and valleys that rolled like waves, I only felt that the whole body and mind heard waves of strong and desolate music playing. It was as if thousands of loudspeakers were blowing the magnificent music of Beethoven, Tchaikovsky and Shostakovich out of the wind,or as if horses pounding hoofbeats of Chinese classical music "Ambush from Ten Sides".

I gazed in shock and amazement at the wonders of nature's creation, deeply shocked by the sight.

The driver was asking us, "Can we go now?"

Several of our first-time guests said to the driver almost in unison, "Enjoy for a while!"

In fact, this is just the prelude to Wanfenglin's movement.

In the afternoon of the second day, when we attended the meeting of the Xingyi Cultural Union Association, we visited the "Xiawutun Manor" accompanied by the host, through the light mist between the mountains, we caught our glimpse of Wanfengling's dreamy countryside splendor.

The magnificent music sounded in my ears again, staring at

totaled 361 kilometers. That year, the Guizhou Provincial Cultural Association had just bought a Volga car; The leader said, "take the Volga, it's safer". Bumpy all the way to Xingyi guest house, when I came to stay, my mind calculated that I had averaged less than 30 kilometers an hour.

Although tired, I was annoyed; It was worth the trip. Just because on the way, I passed Huajiang Slope, and the 72 turns. Now, due to the opening of the expressway, the once famous 72 turns turn is now rarely spoken of.

The movie and TV series "Twenty-Four Turns" let the audience only know the 24 turns of Guizhou Mountain Road, but buried the 72 turns. In fact, in Guizhou, there are many sayings about multi-lane on the mountain roads. Xiuwen County, where I once lived, is close to Guiyang, and the bus has to cross a slope called "seven road turns". I remember several female youth in Shanghai who vomited when they crossed the big hill of "seven road turns" by bus.

When the Jeep kept hanging gear and finally circled up the top of the 72-way Huajiang Mountain, we all heaved a long sigh of relief and repeatedly said, "Rest for a while, rest for a while."

The driver stopped the car, rubbed the hands that had just gripped the steering wheel, and said to us, "This is the first time to cross the slope of the Huajiang River, you can enjoy the mountains on this side."

Following his gesture,we gazed in the direction he pointed, what a magnificent picture of ocean of mountains!

72

# The Movement of Wanfenglin

*Love in the Mountains and Rivers of Guizhou*

Wanfenglin is a World Natural Heritage site located in the hinterland of mountains at the junction of Guizhou, Guangxi and Yunnan province.

With the completion of a county-to-county highway project in Guizhou province at the end of 2015, Chinese and overseas tourists have been increasingly visiting Wanfenglin. Almost all my friends, when they met me, would talk excitedly about their feelings about Wanfenglin.

When I was young, Wanfenglin was still hidden deeply in the mountains of southwest Guizhou, and no one in the culture and tourism industry, neither from Guiyang, the provincial capital of Guizhou, nor Zunyi, the famous city, ever mentioned this scenic spot to me.

I remember the first time I went to Xingyi, at 8 a.m., I set out in front of the dormitory of Guizhou Provincial Cultural Association at the gate of Guanshui Road, and when I arrived at the guest house in Xingyi, it was already past 9 p.m. It took me 13 hours on the road.

From Guiyang to Xingyi, the road mileage at that time

off-site production of the Premier's long-cherished wish, but made a rare wine, "Zhen wine".

Another 38 years have passed. How is Zhen wine now?

We went to the old factory built in 1975, and went to the new Zhaojiagou factory expanded with the help. We tasted the new Zhen wine, and the old Zhen wine. After the tasting, the painters, calligraphers, publishers and filmmakers who went from Shanghai said, "Every day, we taste such good wine, and we can't drink the wine we usually drink anymore after this!"

Accompanying the writers and artists and the crew of "Wine World", I never thought that they would not be too amazed by the colorful mountain flowers, but would be attracted by one Moutai-flavor baijiu after another. Can this be the harvest of my exploration?

distilleries in the town. Even land prices have gone up.

I said not prescient, just because I have a deep feeling with the Chishui River basin.

This time when I came to Wuyou Distillery, I met several old acquaintances from my youth. One of them was Ding Dehang, a friend of Guizhou Youth Federation, who came from Hangzhou more than 40 years ago. Rooted in Moutai in Guizhou, he was a member of the Youth League launched by Moutai Distillery, and now he is a national Moutai master, and a member of the Party Committee of Moutai Group before retirement. After retiring, He and several old friends who had worked in Moutai vowed to reach to the next level. Make the second legend wine of Moutai town, make a good wine that follows Moutai! Their brand "Wuyou", symbolizes a life and health without worries.

During the tasting event, they placed two small bottles of wine in front of each guest and numbered them and asked all the guests who can and can't drink to score. The results were announced, with one number scoring 16 points and one number scoring 14 points. Then the notary announced that the two small cups of wine, one is Moutai, one is the new brew Wuyou. This result informed everyone that the old man made was indeed very close to Moutai-flavor baijiu.

In the book *Secret History of Moutai*, I wrote a section of Moutai Distillery under the direct care of Vice Premier Fang Yi, after 10 years of hard fighting, research and exploration, regrettably admitted that it did not complete the story of Moutai hundred kilometers of Chishui Valley is a truly world of Moutai-flavor baijiu!"

What he said was the truth, we walked into the thousand tons of soy sauce wine base planned and put into production near Xishui Tucheng, witnessed the practice of high temperature koji-making, high temperature fermentation and distillation, and felt extremely magical. This manual operation of the traditional process, literally was a typical representative of Moutai, Moutai brewing process!

Fellow filmmakers, novelists, screenwriters, publishers, calligraphers, and artists were all amazed and praised.

Compared with them, I have lost count of the number of times I have been in this Chishui Valley in Guizhou for 55 years.

I not only came to the Chishui Valley again and again in the autumn and winter after the ninth day of the Double Ninth Festival, but also came to gather customs with the scholars and discuss why it happened to be such a valley area, such a piece of landscape land, to brew the Moutai-flavor baijiu that is now famous overseas. Therefore, at the beginning of the century, the Renhuai Municipal Party Committee and the municipal government, where Moutai Town is located, went to Shanghai to hold a special seminar and made it clear that "Chinese liquor has entered the 21st century and it has entered the era of Moutai-flavor baijiu."

Some people ask me, "how did you have this foresight?" Now just the small Moutai town, brewing Moutai into a large-scale manufacturers, there are more than 360 well-established

# Chishui

## River Valley in Spring

Love in the Mountains and Rivers of Guizhou

In the spring of 2023, the crew of *Wine World* invited me to visit the Chishui River Valley, which is gradually becoming well-known in to the world.

It was spring. The lush ridge and hills on both sides of the river valley were covered with all kinds of gorgeous flowers. The season of apricot flowers has passed, and the pear and plum flowers is booming, competing to bloom the most beautiful colors. And the peach blossoms had just opened their buds there. And the speckled, red, tangerine, orange wildflowers, blinking in between the green so thick that painters can hardly describe them, played the role that they must come every year.

Most of the guests invited by the production team were the first time to enter the Chishui Valley, the old painter Lu Pengcheng, who has been to the countryside and taught in Zunyi area, has not come to the north of Guizhou for nearly 30 years. Too much has changed, he kept marvelling from time to time! The famous director Zhang Jianya, from the first day he came here, said in a tone of amazement, "What a surprise, what a shock! Many people talk about wine town, wine city! This trembled; My eyes were all covered by the snowy waves, foam, beads, tears glare, flying down the wild waves of the mountains and valleys, to the sky, like thousands of tigers roaring and dragon singing.

In the waves of joy like the waterfall sound, I felt like being in a floating fairyland, this was the Milky Way falling from heaven, this was Penglai coming to the world, this was a rare magnificent landscape.

Standing by Chishui Waterfall, I soaked a body of water mist and drizzle, my head and face all wet, but I always smiled, and all the partners together to feel the joy of the beauty of the world.

shouting, "Mr. Ye, be careful, the road is not good, don't fall down."

Fortunately, I was able to walk on this winding paths, and walked fairly steadily. But it's hard work. My two eyes, whole body focused on the walk.

I was really tired. The accompanying friend said, "If were not to fulfill your wish, we wouldn't come to see this waterfall."

I only turned a corner on the steep downhill path and felt a whirl of fog and rain—soaked moisture on shoulders, chests, hair, and faces. This feeling was not new to me at all, I have felt this misty drizzle of water in the Xiniu Pond of Huangguoshu and in front of Niagara Falls. The difference is that Niagara Falls, on the border of the United States and Canada, provides blue plastic raincoats, and the cost is included in the ticket. Shizhangdong Waterfall is free of charge, do not sell tickets.

Almost at the same time as the fog and the rain came, a thunderous wave echoed across the valley. I wiped my face, and looked up to see the snow waves rolling waterfall in the mist curtain accompanied by water pouring down, with its powerful force that seemed to hit the stone through the cloud.

The rumbling of the earth that day was too loud. Nothing can be heard in the ear, my partners vigorously waved their hand, opened their mouth and shouted something. I couldn't hear, and only saw everyone laughing. Acquaintances and strangers danced excitedly.

A song of joy rose from my heart, and then my heart

Later, I became a writer on that land, and worked in the Provincial Federation of Literature and Arts. Each time that I met the authors from northern Guizhou, especially Chishui County, who came to the provincial capital, and in the middle of small talk, I would start a conversation and ask about the Shizhangdong Waterfall.

To my surprise, many people didn't know about Shizhangdong Waterfall. Even if they have heard of it, they would tell me frankly, "Mr. Ye, this waterfall is too remote, leaving the county, there are 70 or 80 miles. If you were coming from the provincial capital, you will not be able to go for a day." In the words, I want to dispel the idea of taking a look at the Shizhangdong Waterfall.

As the locals in Chishui first told us, Shizhangdong Waterfall is quite comparable to Huangguoshu Waterfall. It has a height of 72 meters and a width of 80 meters. When I took the photo in front of the waterfall, I was often asked: Did you take this photo under Huangguoshu Waterfall? It can be seen that this hanging waterfall and Huangguoshu Waterfall do have similar wonders.

I remember the first time I went to see the Shizhangdong Waterfall, I took a jeep. At that time, Beijing Jeep was already the best car in the countryside.

It took nearly two hours on the road in the mountainous area of Qianbei to finish the nearly 40 kilometers of rural road. To get off the car, to see the waterfall, you must walk a rugged mountain road toward the bottom of the canyon, there were guides in front of you, and people behind you were constantly waterfall know it from their textbooks and language teachers.

Chishui Waterfall is not so lucky.

First, the waterfall is hidden deep in the mountains in northern Guizhou near Sichuan Province. Chishui County is a county right next to Sichuan. The Red Army crossed the Chishui River for the fourth time in the Long March to go to Sichuan. The Chishui Waterfall is far away from this famous river. Moreover, for many years, this waterfall has been called Shizhangdong Waterfall in the vernacular of local people.

When I was educated youth in Guizhou, I heard from my fellow villagers that there was a magnificent waterfall in the deep mountains near Sichuan in the north of Guizhou.

I was immediately interested, repeatedly asked, "ten feet cave? Is the waterfall ten feet deep or ten feet wide? Where is it?"

The rural primary school teacher who told me about it shook his head repeatedly at me, "It is so far away that I have never seen it, but I just heard that it is very spectacular!" At the time, I thought seeing Huangguoshu Waterfall was enongh no matter how beautiful Shizhangdong Waterfall was, it could not exceed Huangguoshu Waterfall. If it did, it must be even more famous than Huangguoshu Waterfall!

Seeing my disappointment, he comforted me again, "Think about it, even if it is ten feet wide, or ten feet deep, one foot is three meters, it can't compare with Huangguoshu Waterfall!"

So I also had to give up the idea of witnessing the Shizhangdong Waterfall.

# Chishui

情在贵州山水间

I have written an article *Twin Waterfalls*, which is about the scene and momentum of two waterfalls in Guizhou province.

Unexpectedly, many readers said to me, "We only know that there is Huangguoshu waterfall in Guizhou, where is the other waterfall you wrote?"

Even some Guizhou people working in Shanghai said to me, "Mr. Ye, I'm from Guizhou, why haven't I heard of another waterfall you wrote?"

In fact, I wrote clearly in the article, in addition to the Huangguoshu Waterfall, another big waterfall in Guizhou, is the Chishui Waterfall. As the name suggests, this hanging waterfall is in Chishui County.

Many people don't know about it. For one thing, Huangguoshu waterfall is so famous that, apart from the fact that it appears in the Travels of Xu Xiake, it's at the highway from Guizhou to Yunnan. Drivers all over the country have seen it, and there is no denying the fact that Huangguoshu waterfall's article has been edited into Chinese textbooks, which millions of students have read. Children who have never seen Huangguoshu are reflected in the light, which is not a fairyland, but better than a fairyland. The seven-arched bridge built in ancient times and the cross-river bridge built in contemporary times are like two rainbows across the river, and the colors are constantly changing under the lights. Red lanterns lit up on all the Hui-style brick buildings on both sides of the Wuyang River. On the balconies of the brick buildings, in the Windows, there were shadowy men and women tourists watching us from the shore with interest.

The lanterns in the Six Plaques and Ten Alleys of Zhenyuan town were all lit up, the stars were brilliant, and the lights were bright. Among the sparkling rivers and seas of lights, the most prominent was the Kuixing Pavilion on Zhu Sheng Bridge, which was built for the celebration of Emperor Kangxi's birthday. The pavilion was 15 meters high, and the outline of the octagonal and spire of the three layers was decorated with strings of colorful lights, appearing radiant and enchanting.

Sitting in the bow of the boat, immersed in the splendour of Zhenyuan night, I admired a lot. How could Qinghuai River in lights and oar sownda compare with Wuyang River? Even the Champs-Elysees in Paris, Times Square in New York, and Ginza in Tokyo would be overshadowed compared with the ancient town of Zhenyuan, which has a history of more than 2,000 years.

Oh, Zhenyuan night, beautiful and bright night.

history of more than two thousand years, has accumulated many mysteries! For example, why is the shape of Zhenyuan's entire town shaped like Tai Chi? Known as the Tai Chi Town, is the S-shaped flow of the Wuyang River cutting across the town a natural river, or is it man-made in ancient times? What kind of historical and cultural information do the ancient paths, gates, bridges, walls, residences, alleys and archtec-tual gardens that remain in the town reveal from the brick buildings built along the river?

For another example, Wu Jingzi, the author of *The Scholars*, had never been to Zhenyuan, so why did he make the mountain scenery on both sides of Tiexi more vivid in his novels than the people who had been to? It is precisely because of the mysteries in my heart that on the night of Zhenyuan, when boating on the Wuyang River, I can get that dream-like feeling and feel the intoxication of "suddenly seeing Jiangnan in a dream".

Oh, this is Zhenyuan of the night. With bright lights shining, the clear water of the Wuyang River glows and the boats paddle silently towards the middle of the Wuyang River. The crescent moon in the sky was moving through the clouds, and a four-official hall was clearly visible in the dark sky. Oh, it was the temple on the top of the Shiping mountain and the cliff. At night, the stand upright cliff covered, only hanging colorful four official hall appeared in our vision, it is really surprisingly beautiful. The visitors around can not help exclaim out with surprise, "This is a paradise on earth, a truely wonderland!"

In front of the boat, the ancient buildings beside the cliff

# Zhenyuan

## Night Dream Song

The ancient town of Zhenyuan has a bit of a mystery. Where's the mystery? New visitors to Zhenyuan would say, why is there a modern railway running through such a small town with typical historical features? The answer to this question can also solve the mystery of Zhenyuan.

The most famous attraction of Zhenyuan is the temple of the combination of Buddhism, Confucianism and Taoism in the ancient buildings of Qinglong Cave sticking to the cliff. India's Mahatma Gandhi studied religion here when he was young. In the late 1960s and early 1970s, when the Hunan−Guizhou Railway was built, Premier Zhou gave special instructions that when the Hunan−Guizhou Railway passed through Zhenyuan, all passengers should be able to see the elegant, beautiful and unique ancient cliff buildings on the train.

I remember, the first time through the window of the train, I saw the Qinglong Cave built by the cliff, the surprise in my heart is really beyond words.

The mystery of Zhenyuan is actually just a modern history of the mysterious Zhenyuan. Zhenyuan, an ancient city with a

情在贵州山水间

Zhenyuan Ancient Town

Love in the Mountains and Rivers of Guizhou

Xijiang Miao Village is beautiful, and the beauty of Xijiang River in misty rain is a rare exceptional experience.

Miao artisans make silver jewelry in Xijiang

情在贵州山水间

on the main street, it is dazzling and amazing. At this moment, between trance, I do not feel that this is a village, but a mountain town on the misty Xijiang.

A unique mountain town, a mountain town with the beauty of reality and fantasy intertwined.

We looked for a long time at this rare sight of the Xijiang on a rainy night. The four observers are most relaxed on rainy nights, and their chief task is to keep an eye on the fire on clear days, to report suspicious smoke and unusual fire in time to the firemen who are always ready to go. On rainy days, day or night, fires are rare. But they still stand from different angles, observe the Xijiang Miao Village on the southeast, northwest mountains and even the bank of the Baishui River movement.

In the evening, when we walked into the Xijiang Miao Village, Vice Chairman Li Shengping, who accompanied us, told me that although it had rained all day, the rain was sometimes heavy and sometimes small, more than 8,000 tourists had walked into the Xijiang. When we came out of the observation post and took the sightseeing bus through the crowded, brightly-lit main street, Chairman Li said that more than 3,000 tourists had come in since the evening, and more than 10,000 for the whole day. In the hot days after the summer vacation, the number of tourists exceeds 30,000 almost every day.

Oh, misty rain Xijiang, seems to be telling us that Miao village every day of the year, there will be a swarm of guests to come.

# Xijiang in Misty Rain

At the highest point of Xijiang Miao Village, the observation post is located beside the best viewing platform. Looking out through the glass, the two slopes of Xijiang Miao Village resemble giant buffalo horns, dotted with stars, all shining with rare beauty in the rain and fog. This beauty is like a phantom, misty. At the turn of spring and summer the rain southeast of Guizhou, has been falling for a whole day. This makes visitors feel that everything is wet. However, despite the rainy season, it did not affect people's enthusiasm at all. On the contrary, the viewing platform outside the observation post is full of tourists. They jostled for a view of the distant landscape and stayed longer than usual. Through the large glass of the observation post, I looked far away and saw the whole Xijiang Valley, full of lively sounds and loud laughter, passing through the vent into the guard post. I looked intently, holding an umbrella, wearing a raincoat and a rain hat, of whom have become a special scenery of the Xijiang night. Compared with that sunny evening in early summer six years ago, I only feel that the bright lights are brighter. Especially

情在贵州山水间

Village secretary Jiang Shijie is forty-seven years old this year, before 2008, has been working in Guangdong, Shenzhen, after seeing enough of the outside world to make money, he said to me:

"Xijiang Miao Village, simple scenery, is culture. This is now the consensus. Our Xijiang tourism has been developed, relying on ethnic culture humanistic tourism. There are so many tourist places in the province, the tourists from Xijiang Miao Village rank second just after Huangguoshu Waterfall, basing on culture."

I think this is the biggest change between Xijiang Miao Village and me when I was an educated youth.

The sun rose to the top of the high main peak of Leigong Mountain, and spread the brilliant light of ten thousand rays to the top of the mountain of Miaoling, to the landscape land of Xijiang Miao Village, and to the happy land of this Miao family.

Hou Yanjiang, 37, a farmer who came back from working outside, said to me, "The farmer shop owners outside all believe in adapting to the tastes of tourists. Xijiang Miao Village is different, we want to let the guests to adapt to the taste of Miao family. Sour soup fish, beef, farm stir—fry, glutinous rice, drumcang meat, this is our food characteristics, this is our food culture. We consciously protect this food culture, but also to pass on to future generations, not to be a sinner of history."

Just as it is with food, so it is with building houses. Mao Yu, who returned to his hometown after working in Beijing in cultural design, proudly said, "In our county, there is no such thing as building a foreign house when you have more money. Just because we all know that I am from Xijiang."

Xijiang people eat Xijiang's food, wear Xijiang Miao costumes, live in Miao's wooden buildings, and even drinking and singing the same way.

In the Xijiang, there is a song that must be sung when drinking rice wine, and I would sing it when I was young. The two most famous sentences in it are: Sing if you like it, sing if you don't like it...

This is the wine culture of Xijiang Miao Village for thousands of years, just like their song culture, dance culture, Lusheng culture, silver jewelry culture and architectural culture.

An old Miao man on the wind and rain bridge sincerely said to me, "In our town, not only can't build random houses, but also can't tear down our own old houses. Everyone all knows that demolition is demolition of culture..."

53

my head out.

Xijiang Miao village was awakening before my eyes. God, I don't seem to know her, a thunderstorm in the middle of the night, the Xijiang Miao Village makeup thoroughly washed over, the mountains, the water, the wooden buildings, the Tianba slope, the wind and rain bridge, even the field ridge path, the thin wisps of smoke rising from the Miao village, all seem to be painted by the brush, especially beautiful, clear and pleasing to the eye; Over the pristine forest of the lush Leigong Mountain, the milky morning mist remained motionless, while the lingering forest haze curled around the dense green cedar, transforming like gauze and thin silk.

The sun silently jumped out of the clouds behind the east slope, and immediately coated the whole Xijiang Miao Village including the mountains, valleys, and forests with a piece of brilliance, and the fog forest and haze that converged together changed and rose to unfold myriad scenes in my vision.

I gazed greedily at what lay before me. This is a magnificent view of nature that no one can paint.

This is the morning of Miaoling, the morning of Xijiang Miao Village, facing the stage of awakening and livelying up on the eastern hillside, I once again woke up: Why do the people of the Miao family living in Xijiang Miao Village so revere and cherish the plants and trees and waters between them, because they have followed the law of animistic survival since ancient times. Therefore, when they hear the questions I ask, they will speak a profound truth in their plain words.

nationality promoted the great tourism of Xijiang Miao Village. This blowout momentum of great tourism promoted the great development of Xijiang Miao Village. The development of Xijiang Miao Village, more and more cherish all aspects of the hometown cultural resources.

I looked at the panorama of Xijiang Miao village in the night, and suddenly felt the magnificent stilted wooden buildings stacked one after another among the shining lights, liking a silver giant butterfly that was about to fly. Oh, is that similar to the butterfly mother in Miao mythology and ancient songs?

### Xijiang Morning

In the middle of the night, thunder roared on the top of the Leigong Mountain as usual. The earth-shaking thunder jolted me out of a deep sleep, and in a trance, I could only feel the "rumbling" of thousands of huge logs tumbling down the mountain.

The thunder on Leigong Mountain gradually faded away, and after more than an hour, it subsided. I turn off the light and went to sleep.

It was the chirping of birds that woke me up. When I opened the window, the smell of the primitive forest of Leigong Mountain came to my face. Oh, it was the sweet, fresh, refreshing smell of grassy logs that you can't breathe in the morning of a bustling city.

I took deep gulps of fresh air and couldn't help but poke

情在贵州山水间

and clothing is solved, Miao villagers frankly told me, "Rice is enough to eat, children can get sew a new shirt a year, but we are still poor, relying on pickled vegetables and peppers to eat rice, we can eat meat and drink wine just once a year. Young people go to the outside world to work. When friends come, we offer pickled vegetables, bitter potato wine to welcome guests. When you came back in those years, didn't you still say that our Miao and Dong village had beautiful natural scenery and that people were still poor?"

In those years, more than one person said to me, "Mr. Ye, to work outside, is able to earn more money than the hard work in the hometown, but we are also bitter in spirit! Back home in the New Year, the kids can not recognize his father. Far away from home, being scolded and disciplined is needless to say, missing children, missing his wife, worrying about the elderly, it is really difficult! This kind of pain away from the family, for us Miao who like song and dance, is more difficult to endure".

According to the interview notes I have saved, 96 to 98 percent of the young and middle-aged people from Xijiang Miao Village went to work in other provinces during those years.

Today, in addition to those who have become professors and associate professors, and those who have made rapid progress and become cadres, all the young and middle-aged people in Xijiang Miao Village are employed at their doorstep, living a stable and peaceful life, family reunion and happy life.

County Magistrate Yuan Gang gave me a set of data. The unique, rich and time-honored regional culture of the Miao

Miao's little girl came to refill my water, and I asked her, "How late does this light stay on every day?"

She smiled sweetly and told me in a soft tone that after midnight, about two or three o'clock, the lights would gradually turn off. She reminded me, "Xijiang Miao Village often tells guests that on the western hillside of our town, every farmhouse is a viewing platform; The eastern slopes are full of stages. Listen, the song and dance drama *Beautiful Xijiang* is coming to an end!"

The performance field is in the center of Xijiang Miao Village, I can still vaguely distinguish Miao singing and dancing laughter, sometimes fierce, sometimes soothing. I can even distinguish which is a lyrical song, which is a bleak narrative of the ancient song recounting the creation of heaven and earth by Pangn, which is a happy festival celebration song, which is the love song of men and women... All through the evening I felt less like I was sitting at the banister in a daze, and more like I was listening attentively, and meditating as the song rose and fell.

I recall the time living in the attic of Miao village when I was an educated youth, that was really poor. To put it mildly, food and clothing have not been solved; To put it bluntly, winter can only be dealt with by the government. And every year in the lean months of May and June, we relied on the government to allocate grain sales, food relief, in order to tide over the difficulties.

Even in the early days of reform and opening up, food

there to see when travelling in Xijiang Miao Village?

I say, customs, culture and landscape.

The two peaks on the eastern slope look like two huge buffalo horns. The ancestors of the Xijiang Miao people, who regarded the cow as sacred, seemed to be inspired by the communicating with the soul of their ancestors, and asked the descendants of the Xijiang Miao people for generations to build villages in harmony with the mountains. Generation after generation, the Miao children who followed their ancestors' instructions, gave full play to their wisdom and ingenuity, and through the efforts of tens of generations over thousands of years, they built the magnificent Miao village that is unique in China and unparalleled in the world.

If, during the day, I watched the entire Miao stilt house, the architectural culture of the Miao family, the rural scenery, and the new tourist ethnic customs carefully on the terrace, then, sitting on the terrace at night, I feel more awed by the bright lights, the neon stars, just like the beautiful fairy towers and celestial palaces. The flowing, water, green trees, ancient trees, ancient wooden bridges and the wooden buildings on stilts were reflecting each other, especially like the fairy tale world praised in the ancient Miao songs.

I sat for a long time, until the five or six Beijing tourists at the next table left, until the two middle-aged female tourists went back to their room, until the young couple in the corner left yawning, and I still sat there, gazing at the beautiful scenery of the eastern hillside.

was just starting to get light by the time we arrived, think about how long the road is."

His words made a deep impression on me. Xijiang Miao Village is the last Miao village close to Leigong Mountain, and if you go down the mountain, you will enter the primitive forest of Leigong Mountain, which is not suitable for planting and breeding. Attaching importance to national culture and developing tourism industry, Xijiang Miao village has found the right way and taken the right road.

The bustling tourists flowed through the ancient streets like a crowd exiting a cinema, the constant sound of laughter and joy creating a lively and vibrant atmosphere.

### Night in Miao village

This is not the first time I have experienced the beauty of Xijiang Miao Village at night.

Several times, after having dinner in the Xijiang River, I waited until nightfall, ascended the observation deck, and had a good look at the lights of thousands of houses which looked like countless stars before leaving and returning to Kaili or Guiyang. I have never spent a night in a hostel in Miao village except in my youth, when I lived in an attic in Xijiang Miao Village.

This time is different, the location of the farmhouse I live in is higher and better than the observation deck.

During the day, drinking tea, I have seen the panoramic view of Xijiang Miao Village several times. People say, what is

Mountain, but now they don't do that anymore!"

"Why?" I asked again.

"Too busy." Song Guolun said,

"Who will do the farm work, then?" I could not help but ask, "Every day there are eight or nine thousand tourists into the Xijiang, all of them want to eat farm food, and taste the sour soup fish, so many glutinous rice and vegetables, so many fish, always have to be farmed and planted!"

"The fish are fed in the reservoir of Jian River." The old man, Song Guolun, said briefly, "The car comes every day."

"Grain and vegetables," Yang continued, "are also supplied from several nearby counties. In other words, tourists in Xijiang Miao village have driven the economy of several surrounding counties!"

"More than 700 migrant workers from my tourism company have come from Taijiang, Liping and Shibing, in addition to those from the Jianhe. Why hire so many people? It is that the people of Xijiang are too busy to come!" Mo Shihai said, "In Xijiang, the old have old things to do, and the young have young things to do; Beautiful people have beautiful things to do, and average looking people have average looking things to do. Everyone lives a fulfilling life."

Guo Subin from Leishan Procuratorate, who enjoys photography, met me Xijiang Miao Village, he said to me, "Mr. Ye, in 1982, I taught in Xijiang Middle School. During the busy farming season, I had to take the kids to work in the paddy fields. I got up at 4 o'clock before dawn and drove to the the field. It walking side by side in a long line, wearing a unified black Miao clothing, grandmas wearing shining silver jewelry, the old men wearing the traditional tight clothes of Miao, each of them holding an oil-paper umbrella in their hands, with the rhythm of the drum, not fast, not slow, stepping to the beat of the drum. Onlookers immediately perceived the unique beauty of this team, some of them raised their cameras, and some used mobile phones to shoot the dance steps and images of the old Miao people, and some tourists cheered loudly, exclaiming "Good! What a unique square show!"

Yang, who accompanied me from Guiyang to Xijiang, is himself a Miao in Leishan County, and couldn't help but say to me, "All the elders in Xijiang have something to do. Look, these old people, every day at this hour, walk on the ancient street for half an hour, do some exercise, but also add a landscape to the ancient street. They get tourists cheering on them every day! They are even more popular than the dances of young girls and boys!"

Song Guolun, a 74-year-old Miao elder, told me, "The children in Xijiang are busy reading; The old people now have things to do, jobs, salaries, participation in dividends..."

"Dividend?" I chased him and asked.

"Eighteen percent of the ticket sales will be given to each family in Xijiang. Depending on how much you work, it's a lot of money! The old people are so motivated!"

Yang added, "In the past, the old people were busy farming, cutting wood and burning charcoal on Leigong coming to work in the Jianhe, Kaili, Huangping county next to Leishan County. Mr. Ye, think about it, this year, the number of restaurants taverns, and aritainments in Xijiang Miao Village has reached three hundred and eighty, the people who are also employed, is over seven or eight thousand!"

This is really a new atmosphere after the development of tourism in Xijiang Miao Village. I remember more than ten years ago, I also came here for an interview, at that time, the young and middle-aged Miao families on the Xijiang Miao Village, all flocked to Guangdong, Zhejiang coastal areas to work. The elderly and children scattered in several villages by the Xijiang River could not find a young labor when they had to do heavy physical work.

It's past 3 p.m., and I'm strolling down the old bluestone and cobblestone streets. The crowds on the ancient street are comparable to the Nanjing Road Pedestrian Street in Shanghai. Shops were crowded with tourists buying and watching ethnic costumes and crafts, and the streets were flooded with people from one end to the other, filled with sweet songs and impromptu dances. In wider areas, as long as someone sings, a crowd quickly gathers. It's a scene really called "eight layers of people sit, ten layers of people stand", attracting tourists from afar to stop to watch Miao cultural performances. The electric carts honked its horn and plodded along among the crowds, and the pathway were soon filled with laughing people.

The rhythmic drum beat "bang bang bang bang" cathes everyone's attention. It turned out to be a group of Miao elders, experience the day and night, dusk and early morning, experience the 24 hours of Xijiang Miao Village today. As the Miao song sings: "No matter where you live, it is the same, every place is a good hometown. What a beautiful home!"

### Qingshi Ancient Street

Many Guizhou local people who have been here, all think that Xijiang Miao Village is a village. In fact, there are four natural villages: Yangpai, Dongyin, Pingzhai and Nangui. (Note: This is based on administrative district today. At that time, there were eight natural villages; now they are joined together.) When I came here several times in the past and asked people from the relevant departments of the province and the cadres of the state and county, they would tell me with confidence that there were 1,200 families in Xijiang Miao Village, each with one Miao wooden building, and that all the tourists saw more than 1,200 typical Miao wooden buildings built on the eastern slope.

This time I went into the village committee and checked the household registration. There were actually 1,472 households in Xijiang Miao Village, with a total of 5,668 people. The total number of Miao's wooden buildings is around 1,500.

However, it is said that seven to eight thousand people live in the Miao Village all year round.

Mo Shihai, 45 years old this year, told me, "Only when I was the general manager of the 'Xijiang Qianhu Miao Village Culture Tourism Company', there were more than 700 people

# Xijiang

情在贵州山水间

**Huacai Road**

Xijiang Miao Village, a shining star over the majestic Miao Mountain.

Xijiang Miao Village, a pearl on the Baishui River of the lush Leigong Mountain.

For half a century, Xijiang Miao Village and I have formed a lifelong love bond.

In the early summer of 2018, on a sunny day, I walked into Xijiang Miao village once again.

Is this the Xijiang Miao Village I am familiar with? Is this the Xijiang Miao Village that I have walked into countless times?

Yes, the row upon row of 1,472 Miao wooden buildings, which dare to call the world's ganlan-style architectural landmark, are still majestically located on the eastern hillside, liking a huge ox horn. The road is still paved with stone, and the rich Miao flavor with sour aroma is still dispersed in the air for a long time. But why does it feel a little strange to me? Why do I still feel new, fresh, and a little surprised?

So I decided to settle down and spend one night in Xijiang Miao Village, just as I had when I was young. At least I can into the contemporary food fashion... The planning environment and guiding tourists is like this, and as a result, almost every family of Xijiang people have come back form working away. They are busy hosting guests from the whole province, the whole country and the world, how can they still find time to go out to work?

Oh, four season's string of Xijiang, with its contemporary history of development, is like a song!

To comprehend today's Xijiang Miao Village, you have to walk into the Miao and Dong village and Buyi families in southeast Guizhou, stay there and chat with the villagers, listen to what they say, and read their hearts from their heartfelt words and ancient songs.

I have walked into Xijiang Miao Village more than ten times, after more than half a century. I remembered more than 50 years ago, in 1970, when I entered the Xijiang Miao Village, the poverty, isolation and remoteness left a profound impression on me.

When I entered the Xijiang Miao Village as a young writer on a art collection tour in the 1980s, the solitude of the village also confused me: how could there be only old people and children left? Where were the young adults?

Actually, it's due to great liberation of the mind, not only young men went out to work, but also girls and young wives went to Guangdong, Shenzhen, Guangxi, Guiyang, Chongqing to find jobs. They say it's easy money out there!

I was dumbfounded.

It may also be because of the adventure of a whole generation, they have felt the outside world, experienced the hustle and bustle of the city, tasted cuisines in the city, and realized the value and characteristics of Miao village life: they have unconsciously integrated what they have learned from the outside world into the lifestyle of Xijiang Miao Village. They put the awareness of fire prevention through wooden buildings, they highlighted the Miao flavor in the diet at the same time, attracting the truth.

In fact, not only Langde Miao Village, I have been to many Miao village in the southeast of Guizhou. Such as Miaojia short folk village new bridge, Lusheng village Paika, Xie Zhai Wind and Rain Bridge, Tonggu Village Miao farmer painting, Miaojia hot spring village... They are all good tourist attractions and ethnic villages with distinctive features. However, we can honestly say that Xijiang Miao Village is the most prominent, the most lively, and the most visited by visitors.

Throughout four seasons, Xijiang Miao Village every day is full of laughter, singing and dancing, the flow of people like a tide, such a spectacle, even if contrasted with other famous spots in the world. France is also a place tourists flock, Notre Dame, Louvre, go in to visit the queue, I have also been one by one, but its flow of people and excitement, can not be compared with Xijiang Miao Village. A few summers ago, I met a middle school teacher from the Xijiang Miao Village on the street of Guiyang. He told me that the Xijiang Miao Village was noisy every day, and there were more than twenty to thirty thousand tourists. If you want to visit, you must inform us beforehand, otherwise you will have no food and no place to sleep for the night.

Yes, as a typical Miao village, Xijiang is indeed a case in point. A case study of successful examples.

To understand today's Xijiang Miao Village, we must understand and think from a historical perspective.

To grasp today's Xijiang Miao Village, we must analyze and observe from the characteristics of ethnic customs.

the number of Xijiang Miao Village residents, we walked into the village committee and reviewed the specific household registration.

After returning to Shanghai, I wrote this article based on 26 hours of interviews and feelings throughout the day.

It's not that I was efficient at interviewing or writing. I had connection with Xijiang Miao Village for half a century and have been here countless times.

Not only have I seen Xijiang Miao Village today, but I also know what Xijiang Miao Village looked like yesterday, the day before yesterday, ten years ago, and more than 50 years ago.

It is on the basis of long-term feelings that I wrote *Xijiang Huacai Road*.

For example, the word "Xijiang" means "beautiful woman" in the Miao language, most visitors do not know it.

I thought this article could be written, the county leaders even praised me, "Mr. Ye, the effect of your article, on the *People's Daily*, and *Guizhou daily*, is even better than many people we usually invited!"

I'm glad to hear it.

However, the article had a big impact— the Langde Miao Village, which is very close to the Xijiang River, had an opinion of me. They said to me, "Mr. Ye, you came to Langde when you were young, and we still have the photos you took when you came, why don't you write about us too? Our Langde has also changed a lot, and tourists are coming here too!"

I had to smile with speechless. Why is that? They're telling

# Xijiang's String

## Song of Four Seasons

*Love in the Mountains and Rivers of Guizhou*

I wrote an article *Xijiang Huacai Road*, *People's Daily* published; A month later, *Guizhou Daily* reprinted the essay in a full page with several color photos taken by their reporters.

Provincial readers read it and said I wrote it well.

The readers in the county read it and said, "Mr. Ye, when you come to visit us again, we will invite you to eat authentic Miao dishes and drink rice wine."

Leaders of Qiandongnan said to me, "A true literate like you has a way with words, you see I often accompanied all aspects of the guests to Xijiang, could never write such an article."

In fact, I wrote *Xijiang Huacai Road*, after a quiet trip with a Miao young man as my guide. The Miao young man is from Xijiang, I told him three requests: not to inform the leaders of the travel company, not to inform the heads of all aspects of the county, and to accompany me wherever I went, finding authentic dishes and a general hostel.

My article *Xijiang Huacai Road* was completed with the Miao young man Yang throughout the night. In order to verify

情在贵州山水间

68-level waterfall

5 km away from Xiaoqikong Bridge, there is another Daqikong Bridge, built 15 years later than it. Local villagers say the two bridges are the "Sister Bridges". When I first heard about Maolan, Xiaoqikong and Daqikong nearly 40 years ago, both the villagers and the officials in Libo and Qiannan were full of praise, calling this place a "fairyland" of beauty and an environment where "deities" lived.

Today, this picturesque scene, which only the deities can live in, has come to us.

about, we just found the fun of it. Sometimes, I would take my father's fishing boat and go fishing along the Xiangshui River to Daqikong."

I imagined what she said in my mind, and from this I came to a conclusion: when people come to a place with beautiful scenery, even children can't help but be affected by the scenery, becoming excited, happy, and playing joyfully.

Some people say that Xiaoqikong is a dream, into its dream, people will fly through the clouds, fantasize, and enter a magical state between the true and unreal. At that time, Xiaoqikong was not a bridge, but a breathtaking landscape, which was closely integrated with the verdant peaks and the Hanbi pond which could reflect human faces. Only the word "dream" could describe the feeling. After waking up from a dream, people will have a kind of ecstasy.

Wandering on Xiaoqikong Bridge, I looked across the Guangxi region from Libo, and then crossed the 25-meter bridge deck to look back over the mountains of Libo from the Guangxi side. The two places are densely covered with green forests, the mountains on both sides of the same verdant green, the seven-arches bridge was almost covered by them. Sometimes I wonder, before 1836, when Xiaoqikong bridge was not built, what was this quiet canyon like? Yao and Buyi ethnic villagers living in the nearby villages, how to look at each other across Hanbi Pond?

No one was interested with my idea, and there is no record of it in the existing *Libo County Chronicle*, nor is there any similar record in the eight scenes of Libo.

more than four meters above the surface of Hanbi Pond. In the early morning, amid the birds voices in the forest, I sat on the stone in the quiet and deserted environment beside Xiaoqikong Bridge. In the visitors like weaving, the girls shouted and raised their hands to take pictures on the bridge, listening to their laughter, I also thought.

Here, why do people become so naturally exhilarated? What is attracting tourists who speak various languages to flock to?

When I got to know He Xiujuan at Hong village in Libo, I asked her, "Is it a long way from Hong village to Xiaoqikong before it became a scenic spot?"

"Not short," she said.

I asked again, "So, when you were a child, before Xiaoqikong be came a tourist destination, have you been here before?"

She smiled and said, "Mr. Ye, I grew up in the village near Xiaoqikong, and obviously often went to Xiaoqikong to play when I was a child. It was so much fun!"

I kenw I had asked the right person, He Xiujuan is Buyi ethnic, her answer also told me that Xiaoqikong around the group turn, not only Yao ethnic village, there are also Buyi ethnic village. I asked her to go on.

She said, "When I was a little girl, I would also help the family to pick hogweed and herd cattle, and as soon as we came around Xiaoqikong Bridge, a group of children would put down their basket and pocket knife and play wildly on and beside Xiaoqikong Bridge, and we did not know what it was cards that promote Libo are printed with Xiaoqikong. Libo's literary magazine is also called Xiaoqikong. Foreigners who rarely come here will naturally only remember: the World Heritage site is Xiaoqikong.

Some people say that Xiaoqikong is embroidered out with green velvet, so deep green and quiet, making people linger.

Some people say that Xiaoqikong is green dyed, a real piece of nature jade!

Some people say that Xiaoqikong is a poem, an unforgettable oil painting, and a song that often haunts their heart.

I said that Xiaoqikong is more than a poem, batches of literati and writers came and went, they wrote how many poems, how many praise prose and essays for Xiaoqikong!

Several times into Xiaoqikong scenic area, I saw painters to sketch, photographers to take photos, their photos and painted scenery for Xiaoqikong can be thousands of it.

There are also many lyric writers and singers, sung for Xiaoqikong more than once becoming enamored with its charm again and again.

Xiaoqikong cannot be fully written, painted or sung. For more than a hundred years, on the Qiangui Road, people from the world come and go, and Xiaoqikong are still attracting waves of guests from home and abroad.

In addition to the attractive scenery, what else draws us to Xiaoqikong?

I walked back and forth on the ancient bridge, which is

# The Voice of Xiaoqikong

*Love in the Mountains and Rivers of Guizhou*

Xiaoqikong is a bridge connecting Guangxi Province and Guizhou Province. It stands on the Hanbi Pond and is called "Xiaoqikong" for its seven bridge arches.

Xiaoqikong became so famous that people forgot its original name, "Wanguxing Bridge".

Someone reminded me that Xiaoqikong was a quiet bridge in a secluded part of the canyon.

Before I could react, someone retorted, "How is it not noisy? Listen, the water of the river under the bridge is running merrily day and night. When there is no one, the sound of the river can be truely heard!"

Yeah, the Xiangshui River is loud. It's all about the sound! In addition, Xiaoqikong we talk about today no longer only refer to this ancient bridge built during the Daoguang period of the Qing Dynasty, but to the entire Xiaoqikong scenic spot.

Many people from other provinces, often even can not remember other scenic spots in Libo, they only remember Xiaoqikong.

Isn't it? The picture albums, books, newspapers and business

情在贵州山水间

Xiaoqikong Head Fall

30

Looking at the distance, the 68-level waterfall of the Xiangshui River is like a wobbly, leaping silver chain, dancing ceaselessly.

Waterfalls all over the world plunge from cliff to valley. Only this 68-level waterfall, flows down along the valley from high to low lying in the stream. I do not know how many tourists unknowingly walked to the end of the waterfall, then came back and say "I really do not want to leave such a beautiful place, really reluctant!"

Whenever I hear Chinese and foreign tourists say this to me, I will remind them, "Do you feel the divine music playing..."

I was in the deep silence of the mountains, with only the sound of running water and the song of waking birds.

I really feel the marvelous state of the "noisy stream is still quiet" in nature.

Oh, the serenade sounds was clear beside my body, melodious, dreamlike as a poem. No, no, no! Not just an ordinary serenade, but a divine music.

I sat on a stone with my hands clasped on my knees, and the divine music gushed from my body and mind as if played by an invisible band. I did not know why, the water of the Xiangshui River, this time seemed surprisingly smooth, the water was calm, the color of the water was like jade, and the mountains on both sides of the green layer by layer, just like a huge rich oil painting. The whole Xiaoqikong scenic area, looked like a giant bonsai in front of my eyes. Oh, the beauty of Xiaoqikong is three−dimensional, and the layers of green are different. The beauty of Xiaoqikong is real. I was right there, and I could reach out and touch the stones, moss and water from the river around me. The beauty of Xiaoqikong is also poetic and picturesque, it is said that the most beautiful landscape painting has to be left blank spaces, staying at the bank of Xiaoqikong Bridge, even the blank place also makes people feel overwhelmingly beautiful.

The sky was brightening up, but the sun's light has not yet crossed the surrounding towering and beautiful peaks, and all the colors of Xiaoqikong scenic area were bright.

The divine music in my feeling seemed to be excited, cheerful and joyful under the invisible wave of the baton.

a recent university graduate, and is the first Yao female college student cultivated here in Yao District. She attended my class while at university.

When we got off the car and came to Xiaoqikong Bridge, the tiredness of being called out from my sleep was suddenly swept away.

Criminy! Is this Xiaoqikong scenic spot I have seen many times during the day?

Only in the misty dawn light, the bridge arch, the bridge body covered with dense green shade appeared like a fairyland. The white fog floating on the surface of the Xiangshui River, Xiaoqikong Bridge seemed to traverse through in the light of dawn. It also seems to have spiritually awakened from the sleep of the night.

The Shui man took down the camera equipment from the car, changed his straightforward character, and lowered his voice to me, "Mr. Ye, feel as you like, I also have to work."

With that, he went off to find a angle at which to set up his machine.

I selected a not too small mountain stone. When I touched it, I felt the dew, so I took out a few napkins wipe a few times, sat down on the smooth mountain stone.

From the hillside trees on either side of the Xiaoqikong Bridge, I heard birds chirping.

The sky was gradually getting brighter, in front of the mountains, the scenery, especially Xiaoqikong Bridge became clear.

Xiaoqikong Bridge at dawn.

And I have long been a friend of Libo's fellow villagers of all ethnic groups, and have been attached to this land for half a century. The night before, I have arranged a plan with a writer, who smiled happily and said, "Mr. Ye, it is a deal, tomorrow morning, I will accompany you quietly to the Xiaoqikong, feel the Xiaoqikong when the sky is shining. I have a car."

My friend is an intellectual from Shui ethnic group, although he is also a scholar, but still does not change his cheerful personality. He added to me, "just the two of us to go, I do not call a partner."

I didn't expect that when him said early, it meant before dawn.

I was still asleep when his car honked two short horns just downstairs.

When I got on his car, he started the car and said, "Let's go in quietly, no shooting. From here to the scenic spot, it will take more than twenty minutes!"

Sure enough, the car drove straight along the mountain road, and reached the usual ticket collection place where the ticket hall and the ticket gate weren't open. The friend said, "They haven't come to work yet! We can just go in."

He grimaced as he got out of the car to remove the barricade in his way. "When we come out, it's not too late for us to pay. The county gave me a pass. Don't worry, we will not violate the law."

In fact, I also know the leader of the scenic spot, who is

# The Divine

## Comedy of Xiaoqikong

*Love in the Mountains and Rivers of Guizhou*

In the book *Falling in Love with Libo*, I wrote an article *the Voice of Xiaoqikong*. Why did I descvibe Xiaoqikong as a divine music?

Because this is an unforgettable travel memory of Xiaoqikong.

Writing the sound of the Xiaoqikong, mainly depicts the Xiangshui Water river under the Xiaoqikong Bridge, which brings the feeling to Buyi, Shui, Miao and Yao ethnic groups who live in the nearby and the tourists who swarm here today. The crystal-clear Xiangshui River offers a beautiful scenery.

I call Xiaoqikong a "divine music", becanse it provides a serenade of distant and intoxicating beauty, a unique feeling when I sit beside Xiaoqikong at dawn.

Ordinary tourists, to the World Nature Heritage site, in the face of one linger attraction after another, can only be helpless with a regret of rushing, hurried on, afraid of leaking what wonderful attractions did not see, did not leave the lens.

Even if the guests who stay in the homestays near the scenic spots get up early, it is impossible to find transportation to the

The main entrance of
Xiaoqikong Scenic Area

overlooking or approaching the Xiniu Pond, there will be a charm and feelings. Watching the mist, watching the water color, and listening to the waterfall make you feel that the waterfall is playing a ceaseless song of life — a vigorous song.

Well, just as Xu Xiake saw Huangguoshu Waterfall in the Ming Dynasty, it is the same when millions of people see it today. I believe that many years later, Huangguoshu Waterfall will still stand on the Yunnan—Guizhou Plateau with its majestic appearance and beauty. This also echos a truth in a way:

Nature is the master, we are just passing by.

being able to distinguish it. Whenever this happened, I felt that the sonata has entered a low point, but it clearly still showed the rare beauty of the waterfall. And that melody, had its own charm.

And more often, in the fog and rainy Guizhou, the upstream of Huangguoshu, can always ensure abundant rain and flow. Especially in the rainy season, the grand momentum of the waterfall is difficult to describe in words.

At the turn of spring and summer that year, flash floods broke out in the mountains upstream of Huangguoshu. I happened to pass by the scenic area, just to the door, I heard bursts of booming sound I had never encountered before. The director of the management area told me that the waterfall had turned into a giant dragon, the water was yellow, looking like a big and angry river that rushed straight ahead, so it was closed to tourists. However, the platform for observing hydrology and water potential was still safe, and the director could accompany me to have a look.

How could I miss such a once-in-a-lifetime opportunity? I walked on the hydrological platform together with several members of the Management Committee. Wow, that waterfall surged forth as if a whole river had collapsed, roaring like a furious yellow dragon rushing into the valley, the wild angry waves issued a huge roar. We could not hear anything we said to each other, and we could only express our surprise and shock with our eyes and gestures.

This was really a rare encounter with Huangguoshu.

But on most days, Huangguoshu Waterfall is a delight. In autumn,it reveals the beauty of the fall season, while spring brings its own romantic charm. Walking into the scenic area, whether was rushing towards the entrance. I accompanied my guests to visit Huangguoshu Waterfall. As long as time allowed, I always led my friends to walk up the mountain path at the side of the bend, walk behind the waterfall, and pass in front of the Water Curtain Cave after fully appreciating the scenery of the waterfall. Of course, we had to prepare a rain gear in advance, and when we walked through the Water Curtain Cave, we couldn't avoid a splasf of water. But the fun and joy of this experience gave us a unique feeling. Just think about it: People travel to south and north, travel to countless mountains and rivers, and have watched many waterfalls near and far. But:

When have we ever stood behind a waterfall?

Moreover, when you truly stand behind the waterfall, brushing off the water foam on the face, through the roaring of the water, you can see countless visitors on the viewing platforms from nearby and distant slopes looking at Huangguoshu Waterfall.

Passing through the Water Curtain Cave, even if only once, will become an unforgettable memory for every visitor.

Because I have been in Guizhou for 55 years, I have visited Huangguoshu countless times. Not only have I fully and carefully appreciated the Huangguoshu magnificent plain water landscape, but I have also seen the waterfall in dry season. During the period, there was no rain for many days due to the drought, and the water coming from Dapang River and Baishui River in the upstream stretch reaches decreased. The water potential of Huangguoshu Waterfall was only a large thin curtain of water hanging there, and even the usual noisy sound of water was weakened to the point of barely wrote the *Song of Huangguoshu*, in which I wrote why there is no Huangguoshu waterfall, the regret of Huangguoshu Waterfall. Huangguoshu Waterfall is the most beautiful scenery in Guizhou, and the biggest reputation, why is it not evaluated on the World Natural Heritage while other attractions are rated?

After coming back from the meeting in Huangguoshu last autumn, I felt inspired to write *Huangguoshu Concerto*.

Standing in front of the waterfall in day and night, I saw the landscape of the normal water period which the local Buyi people usually talk about. It is the most ordinary view. Puring this period, the waterfall is clearly divided into four branches, each with its graceful form and character. From the left to the right, the first waterfall has the smallest folow, relatively thin. But because of this, this waterfall presents a clear and beautiful appearance, spreading out freely. The second waterfall shows the magnificent momentum. It's also the core of the whole Huangguoshu waterfall, pouring down from top to bottom with shocking and magnificent flow. Compared to the second one, the momentum of the third waterfall is slightly inferior, and is different from the second waterfall which cascades down majestically from upper and lower. The third is large and is also small, people will have doubts, why the waterfall on the top is so large, before falling into the pool, it will suddenly narrow. Where did the rest of the water splash? By the way, that's how the Water Curtain Cave behind the waterfall was discovered. More than 40 years ago, the Water Curtain Cave scene in the TV series "Journey to the West" was filmed here. The third waterfall fell down from the top to the front of the cave, and half of the water

# Huangguoshu

## Concerto

I came to Guizhou as a educated youth when I was 19 years old and have been connected to with Guizhou mountainous villages for 55 years. Over more than half a century, I have been to Huangguoshu for many times, starting from my youth when I rode in a truck with a c and looked at the distant waterfall from a commanding position. I clearly felt the concerto of Huangguoshu, layered, infinite magnificent and long.

I have published several articles about Huangguoshu in newspapers and magazines in Shanghai and elsewhere. I remember the first article was titled *Huangguoshu Waterfalls*, which introduceed that Huangguoshu is not a large waterfall that people are used to seeing, but a whole waterfall group, with seventeen or eighteen falls. And I selected the biggest drop of Guanling explosion, 18 drops of Nadaguan Waterfall, the widest Doupotang Waterfall and Galaxy waterfall wrote one by one.

The purpose is to tell tourists, after a long time to Huangguoshu, they shouldn't only see just one waterfall, and miss the other beautiful waterfalls.

Later, I wrote the rare *the Rainbow of Huangguoshu* and

Water Curtain Cave of Huangguoshu Waterfall

情在黄果树水帘

At that time, Huangguoshu Waterfall can lead the whole Huangguoshu Waterfall group, focusing mainly on water views; The Chishui Waterfall is characterized by the Danxia landform with steep cliffs and valleys, which leaves people an unforgettable impression on these "double waterfall".

"Double waterfall tour" requires vision and mind, whether at Huangguoshu Waterfall scenic area, or Chishui Waterfall scenic area, you need to have an open mind and innovative vision, in order to do this creative activity.

Some people will say, it's so far from Zhenning to Chishui, can it be done?

Some people will say, I go to one place, and I will find time to visit another place later, can't I?

I have to say, the effect is not the same as the feeling. Travel is all about new ideas, new initiatives.

Think about it, when a trip allows tourists to see two of the best waterfalls in China and even in Asia, when two waterfalls appear in our mobile phones at the same time, Guizhou tourism will inspire people the feeling of innovative ideas.

had its name changed. Therefore, its popularity is slightly less. And another reason is that many tourists who have seen Chishui Waterfall come back and say that Chishui Waterfall is similar to Huangguoshu Waterfall. Since it is similar, many guests who have seen Huangguoshu Waterfall do not want to see Chishui Waterfall again. Besides, Chishui is so far away and very close to Sichuan, why spend so much effort and time?

It's tourist psychology.

The reason why I put the two waterfalls together in this short article is to say that in addition to the similarities between Chishui Waterfall and Huangguoshu Waterfall, there are many differences.

What we want to emphasize is the difference between them. For example, the Danxia landform where Chishui Waterfall is located; for example, if you go to see Chishui Waterfall, you can also see the landscape of tree ferns and bamboo sea that you can't see elsewhere; for example, the both sides of the Chishui River Grand Canyon where the waterfalls are located, a unique style, and its canyon landscape is not inferior to the Grand Canyon. Our Chishui River is a river of drinking, spilling out the famous wine, can wine flow from the Grand Canyon of Colorado in the United States?

In addition to emphasizing the differences between Chishui Waterfall and Huangguoshu Waterfall, I would also like to suggest and call for a "double waterfall tour", that is, to visit the waterfall, to enjoy the waterfall, especially to enjoy the charm and grandeur of the waterfall.

# Twin Waterfalls

There are many waterfalls in Guizhou, but the most famous ones are two: Huangguoshu Waterfall and Chishui Waterfall.

Chishui Waterfall, originally called Shizhangdong Waterfall, is slightly less well-known than Huangguoshu Waterfall.

Why is that?

Many people will blurt out that this is Huangguoshu Waterfall when they see a photo of Chishui Waterfall.

Don't blame these provincials, between the two waterfalls, there are indeed similarities. It's easy to mix them up without looking closely. Huangguoshu Waterfall was publicized early and edited into the school textbooks. It is also closer to the highway, and it is much closer to Guiyang and Anshun, two big cities in Guizhou, compared to Chishui Waterfall which is much farther away. That is why Huangguoshu Waterfall is so much better known.

When people talk about Guizhou, they will also talk about Huangguoshu Waterfall, just as they talk about the Zunyi Conference and Moutai wine.

Chishui Waterfall, however, was advertised a little later and approached the waterfall, what did we see?

Besides the misty and billowing waterfall, there was a gorgeous rainbow hanging over the snow-white waterfall! One rainbow arched across the cliff beside Xiniu Pond, while the slightly lower one seemed to be stretching with all its might to encircle the wat erfall. The longest, most beautiful and most magical rainbow hung in the middle of the waterfall, which was illuminated by the slanting sunlight, making it glow with dazzling colors. The tourists excitedly waved and cheered towards the rainbow, shouting and screaming, and rushed to take photos against it, as if the rainbow of Huangguoshu was a long-lost friend of everyone.

As I stood there, I thought to myself: Oh, rainbow of Huangguoshu, I see you at last.

45 degrees...

Well, it's so complicated! No wonder I've been there so many times and never seen a rainbow! The friend giving the tips kept recommending: choose a morning in the autumn, around nine o'clock, when the sun shines on the waterfall from the southeast Stand in the third, fourth, and fifth window holes of the water curtain cave look towards the opposite bank and Xinui pond, you will see a double rainbow. If you stay a little longer, the rainbow will rise with the sun, and you will see the tourists stand on Elephant Trunk Ridge, as if they are right on the top of the rainbow.

I stuck out my tongue. With so many harsh, exquisite conditions, I think I am not lucky to see the rainbow of Huangguoshu. But deep down, was not convinced. When I visited Arashiyama in Australia, the "most beautiful place in the world" praised by the Queen of England, I saw a rainbow after the rain! My Australian friends said I was lucky.

In the year when the National Book Fair was held in Guizhou, before The Beginning of Autumn, I accompanied the publisher of Shanghai Literature and Art Publishing House to visit Huangguoshu. We left Guiyang early that morning, reaching the newly refreshed scenic area before nine o'clock. The morning mist had not cleared, and there were just few tourists. As we

情在贵州山水间

Waterfall.

    I asked: What are the conditions? First, the weather should be good, to choose a sunny day. When I hurriedly say I have been to several sunny days, never touch. Just having sunlight is not enough, it has to be a foggy time. I have also seen mist many times, the sun shines on the water mist, leading to the transpiration. I could not see the rainbow. I shook my head. Another condition is the angle of view. Rainbows appear when the angle between the viewer's line of sight and the sunlight is

Doupotang Waterfall

12

# The Rainbow of Huangguoshu

I have been to Huangguoshu Waterfall many times. A few decades ago, I passed by in a truck and looked at the waterfall on the highway. After becoming a writer, I was invited back to Great Falls. From watching the falls with guests who come to visit the falls, to spending the night in hotels near the falls; from a thorough tour of each cascade of the waterfall group, to the attractions around the Great Falls; from winter waterfall to spring and summer waterfall; from the waterfall in the rain to the waterfall in the drizzle; from the waterfall in neon lights at night to the waterfall in fog in the morning... It can be said that I already have experienced every landscape of Huangguoshu Waterfall.

However, my only regret is that I have never seen the rainbow of Huangguoshu Waterfall. The tourists who saw the Huangguoshu rainbow came back to describe the scenery when they were beaming with animated face, which tickled my heart and gave me a good burst of envy. My friend from the Huangguoshu Administration Bureau told me that there are several prerequisites for you to see the rainbow in Huangguoshu precious moment.

I laughed, too.

Yes, I have been to Huangguoshu dozens of times, and this was the first time I have seen the waterfall was tied with three rainbow ribbons.

I couldn't help but write this poem. After returning to Shanghai, I thought it over, but I still felt it was not enough, so I wrote *The Song of Huangguoshu* happily.

Readers, don't you think it's time to sing a song for Huangguoshu?

inspired by this that I created the place names of "Sun Bay" and "Moon Pool" in my novel.

Walking along the Tiaoshui River plank road, there is the Wind and Rain Promenade. When visitors take a rest here, they can see the banyan tree park on the right. The earliest I heard of the allusion that Huangguoshu evolved from Huangeeshu trees was told by an old man in the nearby village.

Before getting a close look at the Huangguoshu Waterfall, there is a small Gothic—style stone church with a steeple, built in 1898, over a hundred years ago. It's must—see. Half Street, which I have mentioned many times, is part of the famous Stilwell Road in the Anti—Japanese War, and the transport soldiers of the American army must rest here after arriving at Huangguoshu in the Anti—Japanese War. First, to enjoy Huangguoshu Waterfall to relax; second, to enter the chapel to do spiritual baptism; third, to go further to go over the "Twenty—Four Turns" of the steep terrain, a heavily bombed area by Japanese airplanes. The soldiers need to confirm the safety, the clear road to move forward. A relief sculpture of the American Army's Anti—Japanese War was built beside the plank road to commemorate this period of history.

What surprised me was when I came to Huangguoshu Waterfall, looking down from top to bottom, I saw a rainbow of seven colors, flying across the snow—like waterfall and the Xiniu Pond, one by one, three rainbows!

The tourists cheered and picked up their mobile phones, cameras and video recorders to take pictures to capture this find that the spectacular momentum of Huangguoshu Waterfall is gradually accumulated from here.

In the past few decades, I have visited Huangguoshu dozens of times—on rainy days, in winter, during the day or at night, in spring and autumn. And I was even in heavy rain to enjoy the violent appearance of Huangguoshu, approaching the waterfall in the evening, walking in the morning to overlook Huangguoshu. On one occasion, Anshun TV Station interviewed me live, with the Huangguoshu Waterfall as the back scene. I often told my friends who came from afar that there are multiple angles to watch the waterfall, you can look from top to bottom, from bottom to top, and from left, right, front and back. In this way, we can truly appreciate the charm and beauty of the waterfall. This tourist plank road built today follows the trend of the ancient post road and provide all guests with multiple vantage points to observe and enjoy the waterfall. Along the way, after the Luo Hong Bridge (Bai Hong Bridge in the *Xu Xiake's travels*), the American Army Anti—Japanese War relief, Xiake Pavilion, unconsciously, you will arrive at the Tiaoshui River.

This section of the Baishui River is called Tiaoshui River because the Miao and Buyi ethnic people on both sides of the river came here every day to carry water for drinking in ancient times. The water is clear, and it is sweet and refreshing to drink. On the downstream side of Tiaoshui river is Xiyi River. It's a place where minority women wash their clothes. "Men fetch water for women's laundry", minority men and women do not interfere with each other, do not go to each other's area. It was to the regulations, each scenic spot can only be declared once, if it is denied by the 21 permanent members of the "World Natural Heritage Alliance ", it can never be declared again. The Construction Department of Guizhou Province and the National Ministry of Construction had to withdraw the declaration materials that had been prepared for a long time, hoping to improve the environment before reapplying.

This one thing can not be said to be the "pain" of Huangguoshu Waterfall. This pain has lasted more than 20 years.

Summer of this year, I accompanied friends to visit Huangguoshu. The sun was shining brightly on that day, and the leaves glistened under the blue sky and white clouds. We followed the best route to visit Huangguoshu, down from the Doupotang Waterfall .

This line was a five-feet-wide ancient post road. In the spring of that year, Xu Xiake followed the sound to see the Doupotang waterfall landscape along this ancient post road. His exact words were, "the sound of the waterfall shakes the sky, heard ten miles away." Such ancient post roads are rare nowadays, and the scenic area has protected them and built plank road for tourists.

No one would have imagined that this place was once a "Half Street" full of stalls.

Walking along the plank road, the broad water of the Baishui River gradually narrows, and the water quietly forms a rich and expansive torrent, which rushes forward in a cascade.

As one watches attentively, it is not difficult for tourists to

The issues included Huangguoshu power station, the power station training center under construction, and the need for hidden lighting in the caves, avoiding colourful lights...

Half Street is the biggest weakness. The splashing mist droplets and spray from Huangguoshu Waterfall cause one side of the mountain slope to be shrouded in a thick fog all day long, so that the plants on this side lush throughout the year. This scene is attractive and has become a feature of Huangguoshu. On the contrary, another side of the hillside facing the waterfall is not affected by the dispersed water mist and vapor, and it is one of the best places to view the Huangguoshu Waterfall. The local people came here to set up stalls to sell rice noodles, noodles, Baozi, plums and other local snacks. Especially in 1982, Huangguoshu officially set up a scenic area, with newly built tourist trails, public toilets and hotel facilities, charging twenty cents per ticket. Due to increasing tourists from all over the country, the locals built restaurants, noodle shops, hostels, teahouses, and photography spots in this best viewing location, gradually forming a street. Because all the buildings were built on this side, people naturally called this noisy, lively, chaotic and unsanitary street Half Street.

The two experts, Sanser and Lucas, were obviously impressed by Half Street they passed every day, taking many photos. When they arrived in Beijing, they candidly put forward the proposal of "delaying the declaration". This made Huangguoshu people who were eagerly looking forward to declaring Word Nature Heritage feel lost.

Upon reflection their advice was thoughtful. According

list. The Huangguoshu Waterfall, which is far more famous than these two, has not been declared so far. What is the reason for this?

In 1992, Huangguoshu excitedly prepared to apply for World Nature Heritage status like other famous scenic spots in China, and even invited an inspection team, but the result was counterproductive. After an inspection of Huangguoshu, UNESCO experts left a comment: "Huangguoshu is the most influential waterfall in Asia, but at the same time, the artificial traces are too many and the ecological environment is too poor, so it is recommended to postpone the declaration of World Nature Heritage."

It's the truth.

Huangguoshu should reflect. Sansel and Lucas, the experts sent by the United Nations, stayed in Huangguoshu for three days. At the symposium, they affirmed the great work and efforts made for Huangguoshu's application for World Nature Heritage site, especially emphasizing the scientific value, aesthetic value and significance of the scenic spot as an important example of karst evolution. In the great waterfall, water curtain Cave, natural bonsai Garden, Tianxing Cave, Galaxy Waterfall, Waterborne Stone Forest and other scenic spots, they were very happy to see, smiling and giving thumbs up from time to time.

However, when the car crossed halfway down the street, both experts stopped the car and kept taking pictures. Through the translation, people understood what they said: It is wrong for the scenic area to build excessive man—made buildings.

in ancient times. On both sides of the White Water River, there were no oranges or citrus, but there were many banyan trees. Local people referred to the big banyan tree as the Huangge tree, so before the Ming Dynasty, Huangguoshu Waterfall was called Baishui River waterfall, or Huangge Tree waterfall.

Due to the similar sound of Huangguoshu and Huanggeshu, the name is almost the same in Guizhou dialect. Over time, people got used to it naturally, and the name "Huangguoshu Waterfall" spread.

During the Tongzhi period of the Qing Dynasty, the conventional name was officially written up, the public defeated the minority, and the name of Huangguoshu Waterfall was fixed and spread to the whole China and the world. Just like the poet Bai Juyi in the Tang Dynasty, he was known for his easy-to-understand poems and eventually became a typical representative of Chinese writers. Bai poetry spread through the ages, the name of Huangguoshu Waterfall, also recognized by history because of popular.

### The Pain of Great Falls

The reputation of Huangguoshu Waterfall is so great, but it has not been evaluated on the World Natural Heritage. One cannot help but say that this is the "pain" of the waterfall.

Since the beginning of the new century, Libo in the south of Guizhou Province and Yuntai Mountain in the southeast of Guizhou Province have been added to World Natural Heritage

1970s, during the off-season for farming, when I met several educated youth partners and went there by a truck. All the way in a hurry, there was no pure water or mineral water available that people drink today, some people said that when we reached Huangguoshu, they should buy a few yellow fruit to eat and quench their thirst.

Huangguo (yellow fruit) that the locals in Guizhou referred to were oranges and tangerines.We naturally assumed that when we got to Huangguoshu, the yellow fruit would be cheaper than elsewhere and could be easily bought from the small stalls on the street.

When we arrived at the roadside facing the waterfall, we saw the spectacular waterfall, but we did not see any yellow fruit on the roadside stalls. In those years, there were no designated scenic spots, no tickets were required, and the cars from south to north could stop and enjoy the view.

The educated youth who could not stand the thirst exclaimed, "How strange! We can not buy a yellow fruit in famous Huangguoshu."

Local people laughed and said, "There's been a misunderstanding, Huangguoshu has never had yellow fruit."

I asked, "Why is that?"

Local people look at my serious face, also could not answer the reason.

After several visits to Huangguoshu, including staying with writers near the waterfall on several occasions, I finally solved the mystery. The Huangguoshu River was called Baishui River landscape of Huangguoshu, and praise the wonder of the Loong Palace, the beauty of the Xuan Tang Pond, and the appeal of the Tianxing Bridge. Listening to their comments and praise, I am naturally happy. I also found that Huangguoshu Waterfall they saw was only superficial, floating, and sweep over quickly. There is nothing wrong with that. However, Huangguoshu, as the largest waterfall in Asia, its origin, its history, its changes over the centuries, its cultural taste, we should know a little.

I mentioned a detail when I wrote about Niagara Falls on the Canadian border in my prose *Meet my lover in Toronto*. The 19th century British writer Charles Dickens visited Niagara Falls. If you read his prose carefully, you will find that the Niagara Falls he saw at that time is not the same as the Niagara Falls we can see today. The place where he had stood washed into the riverbed, he could not take the sightseeing elevator, he could not experience the joy and thrill of crashing over the falls on a yacht in a plastic raincoat, he did not have the luxury of sitting in a revolving restaurant with a cup of coffee overlooking the falls, he did not have cars in his day, he went to Niagara by a horse-drawn carriage. Trekking around the riverbank for waterfall views ...

All of this is just to show that scenic spots will change with time. I have written this short article after 25 years, is to inform readers of some little-known anecdotes of the Great Falls.

### Huangguoshu Waterfall without yellow fruit

The first time I went to Huangguoshu Waterfall was in the

# The Song of Huangguoshu

*Love in the Mountains and Rivers of Guizhou*

Twenty-five years ago, when I returned to Shanghai from Guizhou for work, I wrote a short article titled *Huangguoshu Waterfalls* which told Shanghai readers that Huangguoshu is not just the big waterfall that people often see in photos. There are nine waterfalls that have been Opened up to tourists as scenic spots. It is not easy for tourists to go to Guizhou, squeeze out a whole day from Guiyang, go out early in the morning, and then drive from Huangguoshu Waterfall to Guiyang, until night to return to the hotel, there is no time to see other waterfalls. Therefore, I did not begin to write about other topics related to Huangguoshu.

Over the past 25 years, more and more tourists are traveling to Guizhou, especially in summer, and Guiyang attracts many guests from home and abroad with its unique climatic conditions. Old colleagues, acquaintances and literary friends in Guizhou have told me more than once that if you want to come, or introduce friends to come, you must contact me a few weeks in advance, otherwise, a better hotel will not be found. When arriving in Guizhou, guests will go to Huangguoshu for a walk and have a look. After coming back, they will praise the

1

Luoshitan Waterfall

# CONTENTS

| | |
|---|---|
| The Song of Huangguoshu | 1 |
| The Rainbow of Huangguoshu | 11 |
| Twin Waterfalls | 15 |
| Huangguoshu Concerto | 19 |
| The Divine Comedy of Xiaoqikong | 25 |
| The Voice of Xiaoqikong | 31 |
| Xijiang's String Song of Four Seasons | 37 |
| Xijiang Huacai Road | 42 |
| Xijiang in Misty Rain | 55 |
| Zhenyuan Night Dream Song | 59 |
| Chishui Waterfall Carols of Joy | 62 |
| Chishui River Valley in Spring | 67 |
| The Movement of Wanfenglin | 71 |
| Clouds Solo on Fanjing Mountain | 78 |
| The Shortest River on Earth in Legend | 84 |
| Should We Love | 88 |
| Multicolor of Water | 94 |
| Drunk Song of Double Six Festival | 102 |
| Jiayou and Anlong | 108 |
| Ye Xin Wrote Guizhou Landscape | 114 |
| Golden Tuole Village | 118 |

# Love in the Mountains and Rivers of Guizhou

◆ Ye Xin

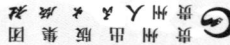